About the Author

Jack Dawe served 22 years in the British Police, he was initially recruited into the West Midlands Police in 1999 where he served in roles that included frontline responder, a detective, an undercover operative and an informant handler. On promotion to Sergeant Jacks career moved from city Policing to the rural county of Leicestershire where he served as a front line Sergeant and Temporary Inspector before returning to his preferred role as a Detective Sergeant on an investigations team.

Jacks career ended abruptly after 22 years service due to an injury sustained in a violent confrontation with football fans. Jack was medically discharged due to this spinal injury and now works as a trainer, consultant and author.

Jacks other publications include his memoir 'Hard Stop' which details his time within the British Military and his service in the Police where he was employed nationally as a Test Purchase Operative who infiltrated some of the most violent organisations in the Uk to secure prosecutions for the distribution of illegal narcotics.

Police Survival guide

There are many publications out there written by ex-police officers on how to join the Police, say the right things in an interview, how to pass exams and of course the memoirs of those who survived their 30 years service in various roles. This book is different, this is a guide aimed at the new joiner who has already joined a Police Force and are nearing the end of their training. Or for those who want to know what it might be like in the Police, maybe to see if it is for them or not.

The knowledge contained within this guide has been gleaned from my own personal service of 22 years in both a City Police Force and a rural County force too. I also canvased Police chat groups from not just the UK but the USA and Europe too. It was surprising how similar the culture and advice was that I received from colleagues across the world, it appears that policing is policing wherever you are, the main difference is in armed societies such as the USA, but this is tactics, the main skills and behaviours of being a good Police Officer appear to be very similar wherever you are in the world.

This guide will explore situations you will find yourself in as a new student officer or as a person who is still young in service. It may even be a helpful reminder to those of you who have been in a few years and find yourself in a rut and you're wondering how to reset the clock and start building yourself again in the image of a proactive and productive officer. I intend to take you through a journey of streetwise policing, we will also discuss the culture you are joining and how not just to survive in it but how to thrive in it.

Although aspects of law will be discussed, this is not a law book. I will, however, encourage you to apply certain powers to situations that will enable you to be a proactive and productive officer.

This guide is not produced in collaboration with the College of Policing, nor is it aligned with any Police Force. If it were, I doubt it would be published due to the fears of these risk averse and politically sensitive organisations. Also, I am not an academic, the advice within is my lived experience, I'm sure I will receive criticism from some quarters, but these people are not my concern. My advice is just that, advice, if you just take one piece of it, then I will be happy.

Ultimately, my aim in this guide is to give you the knowledge and skills you need to survive and get home to your families at the end of each shift safely.

Joining your team

The first day on shift can be quite daunting, you are entering into a new place with new people, all of them know each other and you are just the new student officer. You may be thinking that they will be judging you from the minute you walk in the door, well guess what? They are!

A new team member can cause quite a lot of upset on a shift, the dynamic changes, your colleagues will want to know what you are about, can you be trusted to stand back to back with them in a street fight? Will you get offended at a joke and run off to tell tales every two minutes? Are you prettier than someone who has been used to getting all the positive attention on the shift? These simple things can tear a shift apart, so, nobody wants to inherit a problem child. Some student officers come and visit their shift a week or so before they join the team. I have to be honest here and say it's pointless, nobody gives a shit. They're far too busy to chat with you and they're probably going straight out to a job after briefing anyway, you will just get in the way. I suggest turning up for your first shift armed with biscuits or cakes, this simple act is worth its weight in gold, buy enough cakes so that anyone else in the building at the time can have one too. This will break down barriers and people will be forced through politeness to acknowledge your existence by just saying 'thank you for the cakes'.

You may genuinely not like certain people, they may not like you, but you are there to watch each other's backs and support each other 100%. You will need to learn to tolerate each other and put your differences aside. Teams that come together have a period of 'storming,' 'norming' and 'forming'! This is an accepted team building process where people who have never worked together are forced into doing so, and as a result of the storming and norming they find their natural pecking order and form a productive team that can work together and deliver results. So, if you don't get on with someone, don't let it ruin your day, maybe have that conversation and 'storm it out' until you begin to form as a team.

Hygiene, uniform standards and punctuality

Nobody likes a smelly Police Officer, these things get noticed by both the public and your colleagues, a female prisoner actually complimented me once on how nice I smelled whilst I was fighting to restrain her. You will find characters on your team that have lost their way when it comes to hygiene and uniform standards, they're usually men who haven't washed their stab vest in the last 5 years, you can smell their body odour and their teeth look like a burned down fence. Once you have spent 10 hours in a patrol car with them you will understand how nasty the smell can get.

So, ensure you wash yourselves and always turn up in clean uniform, polish your boots at the beginning of every shift and again during the shift if they get dirty. Members of the public do not want your dirty boots and uniform in their living rooms. Consider how you look when you walk in to someone's life that is in crisis, do you exude professionalism and confidence? Or do you look like a bag of shit? Looking the part is an important part of the job, if you look the part and speak with confidence people will follow your lead, if you don't look the part people will lose respect for you and doubt your abilities.

Punctuality, this is not only professionalism and good manners, but also vital to the effective running of a team, if you are late you put people's lives at risk. One of your team may have to deploy to a call out alone and your absence means they have no back up, this is the same for those who are fond of calling in sick when not sick, things like this puts your colleagues safety in jeopardy. As a rule I always turned up 20 minutes early at least for a shift, this gives you sufficient time to get changed, prepare any kit and grab a brew. You may also be thanked by the shift you are taking off; they could have been on a bed watch with an injured suspect in hospital or at a crime scene all night. Knowing that someone has come on early and is able to take them off so they can go home on time will show you are a team player. If you are thinking,

'I don't get paid to come in 20 minutes early, I'll start bang on time',

then you have chosen the wrong job, the Police is a vocation and being a team player is the only way we survive.

Mindset

Prepare yourself for being on the front row seat of the most amazing show in the world that very few people get to witness(Southland). However, the entrance fee for this show comes at a high price,

- You will work 24/7 shifts.
- You will have to work unplanned overtime beyond the end of your shift.
- You will miss meal breaks; your hot food will go cold when you are called out to an emergency.
- If you start to avoid work you will piss off the control room staff; they will then give you the worst jobs as a reward, sometimes it's easier to just do the job properly, some officers use more energy avoiding work than actually doing it.
- You are now a grown up, you are expected to act like one. Do not involve your parents in your work life, keep them updated if you live with them as to what time you may be home. I have seen parents of young officers complaining to the shift sergeant that their child has missed a dinner break or worked too many hours. Some parents have even arrived at incidents to keep their child company because they were scared of being alone with a dead person in a house. Yes, this officer actually had her dad searching the house with her when the Inspector arrived, you can imagine how much grief they got from management and their colleagues.
- If you are unsure of anything, your tutor is your first port of call. If they are not available then maybe your shift Sergeant or a senior colleague. Do not become an 'Askhole', it's a bit like an asshole but its someone who asks questions just for attention. I had a team member that pestered me as soon as I came into the room with questions and for guidance in investigations, not a problem, as a shift sergeant that was my job. However, it was continual and I knew that the officer was just deferring questions to me as he lacked confidence in decision making, he also wanted my attention and validation. I did 2 things,
  1) I gave him an appointment slot an hour later, guess what happened? he got bored and finally made a decision himself or researched the answer.
  2) After this I asked him what he thought was the right thing to do? often he had the correct answer and didn't need my help.

Whatever you do, do not ask multiple people the same question in the hope that they will give you the answer you want, if you go to someone for advice, take it. If you don't trust their judgement then don't ask them. This is a cardinal sin and your colleagues will pick up on it.

However, do not be afraid to ask genuine questions if you don't know the answer, everyone knows that you will need support and they will give it.

- Remember you are the student officer, nobody cares what sex, age, religion, ethnicity or sexual orientation you are. They want to be able to trust you to protect them and do the job, nothing else, so if you come in with political agendas and think you can use them to gain influence, you will lose friends very quickly, so, get over yourself, nobody cares about your agendas.
- You are the student officer, make the flipping tea! This has always been the tradition and the baton has been handed down from student officer to student officer for generations. If you are one of these people who drinks only water, nobody cares, make the tea for the shift at the beginning of every day. It is not bullying, as some instructors may tell you, it is an act of humility and good favour to your senior colleagues. It shows that you don't think yourself as being better than anyone on the team, they have been through it, so they understand. It gives you an opportunity to mix with your new team, even someone saying thank you is a small step into their trust, some officers will even help you make the tea and conversations will begin and trust will be built. You will eventually learn how people like their tea or coffee, at busy times they will appreciate you turning up with their preferred drink without being prompted.
- Learn resilience and how to take criticism and have a sense of humour, don't take yourself too seriously. You will get criticism; you are learning and the only way that happens is through feedback. Take it in the spirit it is meant, if you take it personal the stress and anxiety of it will just eat you up.
- Biting, this is the art of winding each other up until someone 'Bites', it can be great fun and the victim of this is subjected to some quite harsh 'Banter' until they break and respond with any form of retaliatory reaction. Once they do, the room will erupt with laughter, and you'll be accused of 'biting', nobody wants to admit that they have bitten and they will deny it, which causes even more hilarity amongst those that have been winding their victim up. Your team will also play pranks on each other, this will include you. You may find your cap badge upside down on your hat, or your car plastered in post it notes, just laugh and make sure you get your revenge.
- Spinning and twirling, this isn't prevalent in all forces, in the West Midlands Police it was daily activity. It's really childish, the victim of the spinning may be on foot patrol or just walking through the car park. They will hear 'Excuse me'

from somewhere, possibly a passing police car, or it may be a knock on the window from the third storey of the Police Station. The unsuspecting victim will 'spin' or 'twirl' around to see where the noise came from. That is it, the perpetrator will be laughing that they had 'twirled' you and that was enough to lift their morale until they did it again to their next victim. For future reference note that the best 'twirls' are committed against senior officers.

- Pocket books and Emails, guard both of these with your life. I appreciate that some forces have gone fully digital and the days of a paper note book may be numbered. But if you are still in a force that uses these beware of leaving it unattended, there are some of your colleagues who will derive great pleasure from drawing a large cock and balls into your notebook to teach you a lesson in pocket book security. Yes its juvenile, but this is one of the ways people have historically let off steam, it was also an unofficial way of dealing with what would have been a discipline matter, thankfully this has died out in recent years due to the lack of sense of humour in the organisation. The same goes for your emails, if you leave your computer unlocked you are technically breaching the data protection act as the information in there is not secure. If one of the jokers finds it open they may teach you a lesson by sending an email to the Inspector professing your undying love for him, some will go further and add to the email what sexual fantasies you want to fulfil with them... Don't say you weren't warned.

- If you do feel that you are being bullied, front out the bully if you have the confidence, Police Officers who bully student officers are usually compensating for their lack of ability. If you don't feel that this is something you can do, then speak in confidence with your tutor or your Sergeant. Don't be fooled into thinking every shift is a band of brothers who like each other, there are dynamics on each team that you will not yet be aware of, the good officers will be aware of who the bad ones are and they will protect you.

As a footnote to this chapter, Be nice, work hard, everyone has stuff going on that we will either not know about or understand... so take time to talk to your colleagues, consider how your actions impact on them and where possible be as supportive as possible without becoming abused or taken advantage of by lazy members of the team.

Preparation and planning prevents piss poor performance (the 6 p's).

When you arrive at your station make sure you have all your kit with you, you'll be allocated a small locker, incapacitant spray, radio and any tech like a phone or laptop/iPad if you haven't already got that from stores in training. Be ready to hit the road running, a job may come in during your briefing and you'll be expected to deploy with your tutor. To prepare for this make sure you get a black tactical type day sack as a 'grab bag', something that has all the essentials in for when you go out on patrol. This is something that you will use for the rest of your career as a street cop, however, do not spend too much money on one. Many police cars get vandalised and even set on fire, so the last thing you want is your £200 'tacticool' day sack going up in flames.

Suggested contents of your grab bag

- Crime scene logs(very important)
- Crime scene tape.
- Disposable gloves x 5 pairs.
- A small collection of exhibit labels, evidence bags and knife tubes, roll the bags up into one of the tubes.
- Statement paper and other essential paperwork in case your tech is not working and you have to go old school.
- Clipboard with A4 paper(can be used for crime scene logs too)
- Spare pens x 5.
- Spare radio battery, communications are vital for your safety.
- Torch & spare batteries(cheap)
- Multi tool (cheap)
- Warm fleece.
- Warm hat & gloves.
- Waterproof Fluorescent tabard/ jacket
- Waterproof trousers.
- Mobile phone charger/ battery pack.
- Up to date map book for your area, sat navs are not always updated or reliable. Guard this book with your life, it will get stolen.
- Spare cash in case of a food emergency.

- Vapour rub(hides the smell of dead bodies when you put some under your nostrils)
- High energy snacks.
- X2 small bottles of water for hydration and flushing off unwelcome fluids.
- Hand gel to prevent infection.
- Small pack of baby wipes for when you need to clean hands, face, clothing..
- First aid kit including tourniquets if you are trained in the use of them.
- Pack of chewing gum/mints, there's nothing worse than a cop with bad breath.
- Toilet paper and sanitary items.
- Pain killers, headaches and muscle strains are a frequent occurrence.
- Sea bands or sea sickness tablets, these prevent motion sickness, this is very useful when you are the passenger in a Police vehicle. Being thrown around on blue light responses and general day to day travel is no fun.

These are suggested items for your 'grab bag', you may find other things that are useful too that you will add over the years. I cannot over emphasise the importance of having enough kit with you so you can be comfortable for up to 12 hours. You may be stood on a crime scene or at the scene of a serious accident with no one coming to relieve you.

NEVER put your grab bag on the back seat of a police car, it goes in the boot/trunk of the car. If you have a noncompliant prisoner the last thing you want to be doing is clearing the back seat of the car of coats, bags and paperwork whilst trying to force the afore mentioned prisoner into the back seat of the car.

Your Locker

Your locker will be tiny, there will be some hanging space in the locker room for coats and stab vests, and possibly somewhere you can stack a small hand luggage size bag, but your actual locker will not fit much in it. There are certain things you need to make sure you have in your locker at all times,

- Spare uniform in case yours get soaked, blooded or ripped, you can't go home to change.
- Spare underwear and socks for the same reason.
- Boot polish and brushes, and use them too, they're not just there for show.
- Spare cash in case you have a food emergency.
- A lock if it isn't supplied with one, people will borrow kit off of you, you'll be lucky to get it back.

- Towel and wash kit for when you have been contaminated, or if you just stink, everyone hates a smelly cop.
- Toilet roll and sanitary items.
- Any personal items or medication you may require.

Boots

In the British Police you rarely get issued boots unless you are qualified to work public order duties, these are high leg leather boots with a steel toe cap and protective foot plate to prevent spikes coming through the sole, they are fire resistant and should not be polished as polish burns.

You will be expected to buy your own boots for work, they need to be of sufficient quality to protect your feet from fluids you may come in contact with, stable enough to support your ankles on rough terrain and lightweight and flexible enough to enable the wearer to drive in them or to engage in a foot chase. There are many different paramilitary type boots out there that will fit this description, however, ensure you don't spend too much money on them. If you are first on scene at a serious incident such as a murder or a wounding, your clothing may get seized as evidence. This will mean your expensive designer special forces boots will remain in the property system for a number of years. Your boots may also get contaminated by chemicals or bodily fluids and will have to be disposed of, again, if they're expensive boots you will be very unhappy about it.

Police drivers did wear thin soled shoes at one time due to this giving the wearer a better ability to feel the engine through the clutch and brakes. If you do this ensure they are solid shoes that will give you sufficient protection. I have heard a recent story of a student officer who wanted to wear their converse pumps to drive in because they were more comfortable than their boots! As you can imagine the officer in question is now famous for this stupid request.

Boots and shoes need to be kept in good order, so, that money you saved on cheaper boots can be spent on some polish and boot brushes. Your whole public image can be destroyed by you turning up to a job with unpolished boots on, it looks scruffy and it hints at the fact that you are lazy and not bothered about details.

Fashion, Haircuts and styles.

Historically haircuts were to be short and of a sober nature. However, the world has moved on and people are now given a lot more freedom to express themselves with their hair styles and beards.

My advice for the gentleman is to keep it short and practical, if you grow long hair and have a ponytail or have a man bun it can be grabbed by violent suspects and it can be entangled in machinery, wire and nature, you will also come in contact with infestations. The same goes for beards, it has recently become fashionable for the fat blokes on the shift to get covered in tattoos, have a man bun and a long ZZ top style beard, I think they've watched too many Viking films personally, but, each to their own.

Ladies, if you want long hair then you'll have to do that special weaving magic that you do and Plait it away so that it cannot be grabbed, pulled or contaminated.

Jewellery, no one wants to see your latest bling at work, save it and enjoy it on your rest days. Earrings and ear spacers that stretch the ear lobe make a larger hole, the afore mentioned Vikings seem to like these too, they are dangerous and can be ripped out of your ears leaving you with some horrific injuries. Chains get snapped in violent arrests and rings can be misused as knuckle dusters. Rings can also cause you injuries if they catch on ligatures, it has been known for an officers finger to be 'de gloved' when they are trying to climb up or down out of a loft space. The ring catches on the wooden frame and with the weight of the officer pulling down on it, it rips the skin from the finger... not nice.

One piece of Jewellery that you do need is a good watch, don't wear your expensive Smart watch or expensive designer watch to work. Get yourself a cheap and reliable watch that tells you the time and date, everything else is surplus to your needs. If you break a cheap watch it can easily be replaced, if however you are wearing a sexy looking Tag Heuer watch that cost you a few thousand you will be landed with an unwelcome bill. The job won't pay for a replacement and any damages awarded at court will take a long time to filter through to you, if they're even awarded at all.

This advice also goes to clothing and equipment. Avoid being that guy/girl with all the 'tacticool' kit, it doesn't make you better at the job, it just makes you look like a bit of a Walter Mitty. Where possible always wear issued uniforms and equipment. Believe it or not a lot of development has gone into designing modern uniforms, they are fire retardant and lightweight and suitable for the job you are doing, so don't waste your money on tactical vests or cool looking trousers, they may melt to you whilst you're pulling someone out of a burning house.

You may get an attachment to the CID in your first few years of service. Gents, the temptation will be to go and buy a sharp looking suit, some nice brogues and a selection of silk ties. Or the ladies might buy some killer high heels that look great with the new trouser suit. Don't do it. Your designer threads will soon be contaminated and worn out anyway from daily use in a Police environment, add to that violent suspects, and you soon end up with rips and stains that will render the suit beyond use. Buy a couple of suits from a high street store, one black, one dark blue, a few shirts and some ties, keep it simple, cheap and disposable. The same goes for shoes, you still need a grip on your shoe sole and protection for your feet. Ladies, you cannot chase suspects in heels! If you can, then you have superhuman powers and I will not attempt to tell you what to do.

My advice has always been **"NEVER WEAR A SUIT TO WORK THAT YOURE NOT WILLING TO HAVE A SCRAP IN. "**

Who's Who on your team? A beginners guide to home wreckers, gossips and alcoholics.

People are just people, and a team of people are just people thrust together with a common cause. As with any human being we all have good and bad character traits, some are funny, some are scary, some leave you bewildered that they even made it to adulthood alive. I have listed a few of the characters you will meet on your journey, these are not rank specific and don't think for one minute that just because someone is your Tutor, Sergeant, Inspector or any other rank in the force that they don't fit into one or more of these groups.

Some of the categories of officers I will discuss may make you think I'm being sexist or misogynistic or ageist, that is not my intention. I also appreciate that some of what is written discusses the darker side of humanity, I am just passing on knowledge about the characters I have met over the years, and although these characters walk amongst us, they are rare, and the majority of your colleagues are great people who will make you welcome and look after you 100%.

Home wreckers and predators

The Police Force is an adrenaline charged job full of relatively young and fit people, this leads to a highly charged sexual environment. Officers working on the frontline inherit a perception of living in the now, they experience and witness violence and death on a daily basis, they may get killed at work on any given day of their career, so they make the most of every minute of enjoyment that comes their way. This, however, leads to a mixture of a strain of sex addiction and power in both men and women that can easily be considered a mental health condition. They become wired to take what they want because they can, they don't care about the damage they cause to their own families or the families of their prey. Some of the ladies join the Police because they want to have sex with Police Officers or they have daddy issues and like older men. Some officers are abusers, as we have seen in recent years in the media, they target naive weaker members of the team and groom them for their own sexual pleasure. They will probably be the shift hero too, making themselves the knight in shining armour who saves you.

A mix of this environment and time away from partners during long and unsociable shifts often leads to affairs and divorces. Sometimes it's true love, but frequently it's just raw sexual tension and You will soon begin to see who these characters are, you will hear the gossips speaking about them, you may even get warned off by someone who has already been victim of them or has seen the devastation they cause. They will manipulate you into social situations, tell you a shift drink starts at 7pm when it actually starts at 8pm, thereby giving them an hour with you before everyone else turns up. Or you will see them continually crew up with the same member of the team, they may even go missing on shift together when they are having sex on duty.

Married officers or those in relationships can spend 60 hours a week in a patrol car with members of the opposite sex, they are in an adrenaline charged environment, relationships build, problems are discussed in their relationships, a bond forms and at times, urges are acted on. I have known of Police Officers with multiple secret relationships going on in the same team, a love triangle which eventually breaks and sends a whole team spinning into division and disorder. Avoid getting entangled in these shenanigans, especially as a student officer, if you get a name for yourself as a home wrecker or just a poor sexual reputation in general this will follow you for your whole career, especially the ladies, men fare better and are chalked up as players, the ladies unfortunately get tarred with a label that sticks with them. I knew of one female officer who had a drunken sexual encounter with a detective in the Police bar when she was a student officer, she was an amazing cop, but people still gossiped about this up until she retired from the force after 30 years' service.

Don't be fooled into thinking that this is just a straight white male predator thing. I have dealt with some horrific cases of domestic violence, stalking and harassment where the perpetrators are females and same sex couples. Do not be afraid to challenge bad behaviours within diverse groups, a victim is a victim no matter what their sexual orientation is.

Thief takers

These are by far a minority of Police Officers you will meet; this is a label that every cop aspires to be known by. A thief taker is known as such due to their propensity for frequent quality arrests and convictions. They are out there every shift doing what we all joined to do, locking up the bad guys. They come in early to prepare their uniforms and equipment, they try their hardest to get the best, fastest and most reliable vehicle to aid in their pursuit of offenders. They keep fit and have an air of arrogance about them, a swagger of confidence that comes from knowing they can take on the baddest people in society and come out on top with a suspect in handcuffs.

They can do this successfully because they know their streets, they know the criminals, they know who is wanted on warrant. These are the elite proactive team officers and potential Sergeants of the future and fall into an unofficial leadership position on the team. If there is a problem that needs solving or a dangerous suspect needs hunting down, these are the guys that the management call in a, 'break glass in case of an emergency' scenario. Sometimes they can push the boundaries of the law to achieve their goals, they are not being corrupt, they stay within the law, but know enough about their powers that they can be creative and apply those powers to a successful arrest. Use these guys as your mentors and role models on the team.

The team hero, aka the cock of the team

Not to be confused with thief takers, these cops started out in life with a lot of the qualities of the thief taker, but they became corrupted by their own arrogance and became lazy, or they abused the title of thief taker for their own gain. Because of their early abilities they often earned the right to become an area car driver, this meant taking young female student officers out on fast car chases and adrenaline fed arrest missions, the girls couldn't resist them and before long yet another sexual conquest was added to their list of naïve female student officers.

The team hero will also not want to get involved in the details of Policing, their pen will rarely leave their pocket and they will drift around avoiding menial jobs that are beneath them. However, when there's a chance to shine out as a hero, they will be there strutting along and making sure everyone knows they are there. After the action they will sink into the background and avoid any paperwork, leaving it to the student officer, saying something like, 'It's good for your development'.

The team heroes homelife is usually a complete car crash too, they usually have an alcohol or substance dependence, failing relationships, multiple ex-partners and have made a multitude of poor life decisions. These people are a ticking time bomb that if left to their own devices will fall foul of the Professional Standards Department. I have seen many cops like this lose their jobs for dishonesty, corrupt activity and domestic violence. They begin to think they are untouchable but they get a harsh reality check when they are investigated and are sacked or required to resign.

Virtue signalling career cop

These are by far the most exhausting people you will have to work with, they will usually be very sociable and agreeable to start with, they are astute and they build a layer of allies around them at all times. Their uniform will be adorned with a multitude of badge's and pins displaying allegiance's to diverse groups, rainbows, autism badges, you name a group on the diversity scale, there's a good chance they have a badge to cover it. Some who wear these badges belong to those diverse groups and have a genuine allegiance, I'm not talking about them. I'm referring to those who are doing it to virtue signal and use it as a vehicle to career progression. I knew of one officer who was desperate for promotion, they knew that the Chief Superintendent in charge of the station was gay, so they decided to join a gay police network and pretended to be gay to enhance their chances of promotion, unfortunately for them they were well known as a straight 'Home wrecker' and their plan failed. There are also supervisors who will frequently be away at conferences or meetings of support to a diverse network. The problem with this was it leaves their team without supervision, so work never got signed off or closed, staff welfare and investigations their team were conducting fell to other supervisors due to their absence. They don't care, they are climbing the promotion ladder and being a good Police Officer or Sergeant has nothing to do with promotion. To get promoted you have to be politically aware and be noticed by the right people, and the right people, aka 'king makers', are usually at these meetings doing their own fair share of virtue signalling to enhance their own profile. The virtue signaller knows this very well and they will sacrifice their teams welfare to achieve their aim of promotion, nobody will challenge them, because if they did they may themselves be labelled as racist, homophobic, misogynistic or whatever diverse group stood for hater.

Plodders

These are the back bone of the Police force and by far the majority that you will encounter. These are competent and mature officers who turn up every day of their career and do their job. Plodders, Plod, or old plod is a slang name derived from Enid Blyton's children's books with a Police character called PC Plod, Plodding along refers to walking the beat slowly and methodically and getting the job done. These officers are satisfied to serve their whole career as a Police Constable and have no interest in the politics and BS that goes with promotion. The Plodders are usually slightly more mature and have stable families and commitments away from work to focus their minds. They will not break any records, nor will they virtue signal their way through situations, they are more likely to roll their eyes in annoyance at characters who do and give them a wide berth.

What the plodder will do is turn up every day, have very few sick days, support everyone around them, be a good point of advice and mentors to younger team members and they will rarely bring grief or upset to the team.

The team mum and dad

These are usually plodders too; they are usually older and have grown up kids and they gain the title of shift mum and dad due to their parental behaviours towards the team members. They will organise day trips, meals out and orchestrate planned sit down 'hot food' for the team on a late shift. If something needs organising they will be there sorting it out, it may be a collection for an officer who is retiring, or supporting team members who are struggling with the stresses of the job, a shoulder to cry on. If you ever have a problem, go to these people, they will fight your corner against bullies, know the best course of action and usually have direct access to a supervisor or support network that can assist you.

The pregnant one

There is a very good chance that you will have one or more ladies pottering around the station in maternity wear. I supervised one station where we thought there was an exploding pregnancy chair, there were 5 officers pregnant at the same time, we had next to no female officers capable of deploying onto the streets. The Police quite rightly protects our colleagues who find themselves pregnant, the risks of letting them out to a public facing role and facing the potential of daily violence are too high to consider as safe. In the early stages they will help with clerical work and general enquiries over the phone, it is in some cases possible for them to take statements from witnesses, but this has to be carefully risk assessed. If you find yourself pregnant, do not hide it because you think you are letting people down. I know you want to support your team and want to be out doing Police work, but losing a baby is one of the most traumatic things that can happen to a human being, is it worth risking an unborn babies life for the sake of locking up a shop lifter?

Gossips, back stabbers and fake friends

A Police Station is a community of its own where everyone knows everyone and all their business. Gossip is like a currency that is traded and spread around like wildfire. If anything is happening in your life you may as well just put it on the notice board; If someone was having an affair, everyone knows about it! If someone had been in to see the superintendent for a bollocking, everyone knows about it!

Most gossip is harmless and is just a way of passing time in the smoking area, or on a long night shift. It may be speculation about a flourishing romance or the drunk antics of someone at a drinks event, or someone who is making moves to get promoted, nothing too serious. However, there are some officers who delight in the misfortunes of others and love the power of knowledge about someone else's life. It is not uncommon for a feeding frenzy from these quarters when someone drops in the shit. Let's say for example an officer has been arrested or is under investigation, the gossips will blow all the information out of proportion and embellish half-truths in an attempt to assassinate someone's character. This can even manifest into more complaints against the officer under investigation as the gossip wants to spread their tales. The only reason I can think of for this vindictive behaviour is because the gossip is using others failings to hide their own insecurities and failures, a kind of, look at them failing, not me, who is also failing, kind of situation. These people are career enders, it's bullying and it can drive their victims to the point of suicide. Avoid joining in on the feeding frenzy and concentrate on your own reputational control. If you live by gossip there is a good chance it will be reversed on you at some point and you or your career may die by gossip.

Also be aware of over friendly creeps who no one else wants to work with, they will make a beeline for a new joiner. Ask yourself why people won't work with them? Is it because they're work shy, or they're scared to get stuck in and won't use force when required, or they may just have bad hygiene? Just remember, there is a reason no one wants to work with them.

The sick lame and lazy...or genuinely broken?

Sickness in any organisation is one of the hardest things to manage, there are so many variables, is it just flu or is it an on duty injury? Has the person caused their own injury or illness through neglect of their health or extreme sports? Some people just decide in the morning not to come in and want to take a duvet day. The duvet day people are dangerous and are not team players, they make the team short staffed and that will mean more work and pressure on the team, it may also mean that someone has to attend a job with no back up. If you are sick, no problem, but if you are the type of person to go off sick because you fancy a day or two off, then you lack the resilience and commitment to your team and you have no place in the Police.

Officers who frequently take time off can be suffering from stress, alcoholism or their life at home is falling apart and they just cannot cope with being at work. If you identify someone like this, or feel that this may be happening to you, then consider getting help, there is no shame in admitting you are struggling and a good supervisor will be able to signpost you to support or be able to set a strategy with your work load to make it more manageable.

Avoid moaners, my biggest frustration when I joined my first team was a hardcore of cops who sat around for the first hour after briefing to moan, the irony was that they were moaning that they didn't have enough time to get their work done.

Avoid the pity parties too, they are toxic! For example, if you have a number of officers who are on restricted duties for mental health reasons, they can begin to bond together in an unofficial peer support group. Each person will have their own individual issues, but when put together with others with similar issues things begin to magnify; paranoia sets in that the organisation is out to get them, their supervisors are labelled as bullies because they have placed them onto a return to work plan. Although we should always support our colleagues we must also be aware of not being dragged into their mindset and we must consider the demoralising and divisive impact on the team as a whole if we do. These officers are probably suffering due to the stresses of Police work, home life or maybe a specific incident sent them over the edge, understand this and support them, don't leave them out of things and include them in everything that you can, such as social events, meal times or finding solutions to problems. Just be aware that in their state they can interpret the smallest act as a personal attack on them and they may start resenting the people around them. As a Sergeant I frequently supported colleagues through mental health problems, if they ever lashed out, I did my best to reassure them that I was there to support them and I never took their complaints about me to heart, it was part of their condition and something I had to expect.

I wonder which one of these groups you will eventually fall into? Look back at this chapter every six months, if you see a pattern emerging it may be time to step back and recalibrate before things go too far. It's never too late to make a fresh start, it's your career and your reputation.

Proactive patrol

Patrol is the bread and butter of your job, and it is what most people join to do, hunting down criminals and protecting the vulnerable. Sir Robert Peel stated that,

'The test of police efficiency is the absence of crime and disorder, not the visible evidence of police action in dealing with it.'

So, if you find yourself running from job to job and constantly taking reports for crimes, your force or department is failing. You did not join the Police to become an administrator or a crime recorder, but sadly this is where the service has found itself, a slave to recording data and statistics. In this chapter we will explore strategies and tactics you can use to optimise your time in fighting crime and disorder in your community.

Know your area and know your criminals

The first part of every duty you start will normally consist of a briefing, an experienced officer or an officer of rank should be briefing you on current threats, incidents of note in the past few days and wanted suspects. They must also be allocating crewmates to people if there is no policy of single crewed officers, you may also be allocated tasks for the day. You can enhance your knowledge of these subjects yourself by reading the briefing pages on your force internal website which contains this information too, getting an in depth knowledge of who is who and what is happening is key to you planning your days activities. However, this is no replacement for getting out of the station and getting in amongst the community where you will gather the best knowledge about what is going on and who is doing it.

When you leave the station which way are you going to turn? If you have no plan when you leave the station then you will be less efficient, there is no point in patrolling night time burglary hot spots at 10am for example. This is the point where you decide if you are going to be a slave to the radio or a proactive police officer who finds their own work. The control room will have a stack of jobs that they are just waiting to dish out, they're usually crappy jobs that will take up your day and produce very little impact on local crime, you will just spend the day being a crime recorder and not a crime fighter. If you can sneak out under the radar of the control room, do so with a plan and with a suspect that needs to be targeted. Get an arrest of a wanted suspect early on into your day and you will not be criticised, it's your job after all, you may get a few grumbles from some people who have become slaves to the radio and only do what they are sent to by the control room, but do not worry about the opinions of sheep, you are a crime fighting lion and you will be recognised as such.

You will begin to build relationships with criminals and their families if you work the same area long enough, you will know them by their first name and you will know their dates of birth and home addresses. You will speak with their family, know who their criminal associates are and where they hang out. This will allow you to plan your patrol to enable maximum exposure to the criminal, if I know they hang around with a certain person on a certain street corner, I will ensure I pass by there. I will stop the car and get out and speak with them, this doesn't have to be adversarial, it can be a friendly chat, a bit of banter maybe. The criminal will either interact with you or blank you out, if they blank you out this will be because they do not want to be seen speaking to the police from fear of being called an informant or they may be wanted on warrant or for a crime, you must run their details through the Police computer on every interaction. Use these interactions as intelligence gathering. If you have grounds, do a stop search, if you don't have grounds take note of what they're wearing, who they're with, what vehicles they are using. Patrol is not just about arrests it's about intelligence gathering too, the information you record and submit as intelligence can assist in filling the gaps in an investigation. Your presence at that street corner may have stopped someone becoming a victim of crime, the criminal will be thinking about your interaction and decide not to commit a street robbery that night because of it.

In a world of political correctness we are told not to stereotype people, don't pre-judge them. I do not believe in this, stereotypes are there for a reason, your mind and body is hard wired to identify a threat in a split second and prepare your body for fight, flight or freeze reactions. So, if you see a scruffy looking grown man in a tracksuit, riding a mountain bike with a plastic bag on the seat in a burglary hot spot, don't feel guilty about stop searching him, there is a very high chance that he is a 'wrong un' and there to commit a crime. There are too many stereotypes to mention but I have found that using them in a proactive but professional way will usually get you a result. I must note though that your stereotyping of people is your brains early warning system, not a licence to unfairly target people.

Don't piss off the control room

Even though you may be out looking for a suspect or patrolling an area of anti-social behaviour, you must not ignore the control room, you should also not try and 'BAT' jobs off. This is a term that officers use to describe the act of getting rid of a job with minimal work and effort involved. Some people become a master at this skill and unless done properly it can lead to you getting a bad reputation and you may face charges of neglect of duty. If you spend too much time swerving work or just generally get identified as being lazy, the control room will be on your back. They will allocate you to every crappy job that comes in; neighbours arguing over parking, it's coming your way, crime scene duties or hospital bed watch of a suspect, it's coming your way. Manage your relationship with the control room, visit them if you are at headquarters, take some cakes or biscuits and spend ten minutes with them and take interest in what they do. This will be rewarded with a good relationship and an apology if they do have no choice but to send you to that crappy job because there is no one else left available.

Thief taking and the thrill of the chase

I have already discussed what a thief taker is and how they conduct themselves in an earlier chapter. The main key to becoming one of these is to make quick and appropriate decisions that are within the law. You may be pushing the limits of your powers of arrest and powers of entry but you are staying within the spirit of the law. I do not encourage anybody to break the law or falsify some evidence just to make an arrest, it's just not worth it! You will know you've done it; others may suspect you've done it, and the criminal and their associates will definitely know you have done it. You will have to live with the guilt of knowing what you have done and with most people it will have a detrimental effect on their values, if you're not the kind of person to feel this guilt, then I'd say you're in the wrong job and a prison cell is awaiting you.

So, what's the problem with criminals knowing that you have lied? Well, they talk to each other, word gets around and in a short time your name is known on the streets as being corrupt. Believe it or not criminals do trust the Police and often come running to us when they are in trouble with other criminals or angry victims, they too need our protection and if this belief that we are the good guys is eroded by corruption they will no longer trust us.

Why do we need their trust? Almost all of the intelligence the police obtain is from the community, either from criminal informants or contacts in the community who know and associate with criminals. If they think you are dishonest or untrustworthy they will not pass on the information. As an extreme but likely example, imagine you are outnumbered and being subjected to a beating from a gang, a criminal who trusts you may stop it from happening, or at the very least not join in. If however they hold a grudge because you lied about them and sent them to jail, you can expect a size 9 boot to the head. Let's not also forget that these guys are often criminal informants too, they will pass on information about your conduct to intelligence source handlers who will be duty bound to pass this information onto professional standards.

Don't be afraid of criminals, just treat them firm and fair, if you don't get them for one crime, another one will be committed soon enough, and they will get caught, crippled or killed whilst in the act of doing it.

Expeditious investigations

When you are sent to record a crime, deal with it expeditiously, don't waste time chasing a job that is going nowhere, if you don't your crime investigations will keep mounting up until they are unmanageable and out of control. If there are no suspects, no witnesses, no viable lines of enquiry then tell the victim that the matter will be reviewed by a supervisor and most likely filed as undetected. If you do not manage the victims expectations you will fail them and they may be left dissatisfied and confused when the matter is filed 3 months later anyway. This will also save you a lot of time, you will not need to take multiple statements from people who have seen nothing or cannot add any value to the investigation, especially if the victim is declining any Police action. If you are filing something make sure you write a working sheet with sufficient grounds for your supervisor to make a decision. If you don't you may end up being tasked to interview or take statements from multiple people before that supervisor will make a decision. Some supervisors are just made that way, they cannot make a decision, they will send you on fools errands and demand 10 statements to make a decision, if your supervisor is like this, I pity you, I have seen the destruction and agony they bring to their teams.

Expeditious investigations are also about taking positive action. Some people may not agree with me here, but I hate to see an investigation with a named suspect, that is taking weeks or months to lead to an arrest. If you get called to an assault for example, the suspect has injuries and are in fear of further attacks or harassment then an arrest must be made that day! Take a statement, take some injury photos, quick check for CCTV at the scene and then go and lock the suspect up on suspicion of Actual Bodily Harm (ABH). You can justify the grounds for arrest as necessary to prevent further attacks and to protect witnesses as well as the fact it is an expeditious investigation and you are securing evidence by questioning, you may even need to seize clothing and search properties for evidence of a weapon, if you delay, clothing can be washed and weapons discarded. You do not need to build a full Crown Prosecution Service(CPS) court file with statements from doctors detailing the injuries at this stage, that can come later. This will cause unnecessary delays and your victim will begin to lose faith and may even withdraw from the process. I understand why people do front load investigations, they do it so that a decision on charging can be made there and then by either a supervisor or the CPS. But this does not serve the needs of the victim, they are left seeing the suspect walking past their house every day, or they receive harassment and threats. If you can get them in custody early, the evidence is fresh, and it can be attributed to the suspect, they may have photos or messages relating to the incident on their phone which you can also seize. Once they're arrested and interviewed, try and get an in custody decision for charging, a threshold test, and always consider if a remand in custody is the best course of action for the victim. If you do need to release them under investigation pending further evidence consider the use of Domestic Violence Prevention Orders/Notices or bail conditions, you still have control of the suspect, they will know that if they intimidate a witness or victim that they will get dragged back into custody again and face further charges...**don't delay, act today!**

Manhunt

Here is an extract from another publication of mine by the title of 'Hard Stop', in this I discuss the thrill of the hunt when pursuing criminals, this is by far the best part of patrol or proactive duties.

If you don't like the thought of hunting innocent animals then hunt guilty men! There is no thrill that compares to chasing down a human being, a 'wanted man' or 'Bandit' as I like to call them. I don't mean like the big cases you see on TV where you have large murder teams with endless budgets for forensic psychologists and other expensive police voodoo, I have worked on murder cases and they are boring! You mostly work through hours of house to house enquiries or sit viewing days of CCTV footage in the hope of identifying a grainy image of a suspect, these enquiries involve a lot of paperwork and a lot of waiting around. The suspects in these cases are usually a normal person who has never been in trouble with the Police, that is until the day they crack and shove a knife through their partner's chest. They usually get stopped at the airport having emptied their bank account for cash, but stupidly used their credit card to pay for the flight they hoped to escape on. Now don't get me wrong there are some great teams out there that specialise in this field, especially in the Metropolitan Police and National Crime Agencies, local Police Forces across the country frequently have murderers they have to hunt down, some suspects do take years to catch and resources from across the world are used to locate and trace some really evil people.

However, my manhunts were on the streets where I hunted down desperados that were Burglars, Robbers, drug users and at times to be fair I hunted a few Murderers too. In my mind there are 2 categories of manhunt.

A street level manhunt can be compared to a rough shoot where pigeons are hunted! The police will see a suspicious character and try to stop them, there will be a car chase of an unknown 'Bandit' who is probably just wanted on warrant or holding some drugs. They will crash the car and a foot chase begins, you're fence hopping across back gardens and sprinting through alleyways, you send up the police helicopter, call for the Police

Dog and direct resources to cut down their escape routes until you find them in a ditch screaming with the sharp end of a 200lb German Shepherd Dog hanging off their arm!

Or it can be the more quality game, a deer hunt where you have a high quality beast with heightened senses and the ability to blend into their surroundings, they have spent years evading the hunter and know the land and where to hide, one whiff of you and they disappear. You have to stalk your prey, know the ground and where they are likely to go for sustenance or shelter, locate the deer, set your killing ground, get the creature in your sights, judge the wind and just at the right moment take the shot to take out that beautiful stag that has been alluding you for so long... After you have caught your stag you can often feel regret that the chase is over, something is now missing from your life and you feel a void where you once had a purpose!

I love nothing more than being out on my own or with a small team with the minimum of support and no supervision whilst hunting a human being who is on the run. It's crude, it's rude and it's a dirty business where time and pressure on the 'Bandit' and his family wears them down. Wake grandma up at 5am every day for a week saying you're looking for their grandson or visit his sister's house as she's getting the kids ready for school, and soon enough the family will turn on the fugitive and they will hand themselves in, or they will be turned in by the family who are sick of the Police attention. Put surveillance on their mum's house and soon enough they will turn up for food and clean clothes! You can then enter the house without a warrant and arrest them! If they avoid their family you target their associates, pull cars over with their friends in, visit their best mates house at 5am and let him explain to his Mrs why the cops are calling at their house. You can visit their favourite pub, even their dealer, eventually you piss them all off...It's all about grinding the bandit down so that life on the run is so hard that they are always on the edge and looking over their shoulder. They can't maintain that level of pressure for long, it breaks down their resilience having to live with no safe shelter, no food and possibly suffering with a drug addiction. Eventually they make a mistake, they get caught, or it becomes too much and they walk into the nearest police station and hand themselves in.

This all taps into their hierarchy of needs which is a psychological theory that shows we as humans have basic needs. If you remove any of these from that person they will not perform as well, or even in extreme circumstances survive as well as the person with that structure. These are demonstrated in a pyramid with 5 levels with 1 at the base and 5 as the peak.

1. Physiological needs like Shelter, warmth and food.

2. *Safety needs like personal security, health, resources and employment.*
3. *Love and belonging, having family and relationships.*
4. *Esteem and respect, recognition and freedom.*
5. *Self-actualisation where you have reached your goals in life and are happy and settled in what you do and who you are.*

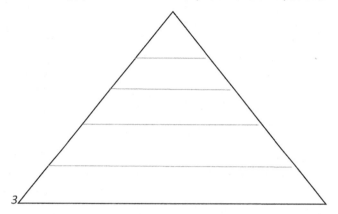

So if you are a fugitive on the run you can forget about the last 4 of these as you are on the run and maintaining those in the absence of your physiological needs is impossible. All your time and efforts will be concentrated on point 1. You need somewhere warm to rest where the Police won't come, you have no money for food, and you know if you go to family there is a good risk that the Police will catch you there. If you decide to commit crime to feed yourself you are putting the odds of being caught even higher, and if you sleep in a derelict building you are at risk from the landowner discovering you, or you may encounter other criminals who may attack you and take what little you have. This constant drip will break down any fugitive and can also be translated into other crisis situations like someone being evicted, losing a job or a divorce where one of the parties is left with nowhere to live and no resources. Everything stops until you get at least points 1&2 under control! (Ref: Maslow's theory of hierarchical needs)

NEVER use the Q word

There is a word that begins with Q, it is used to describe a time when there is no radio traffic on your handset, the public are behaving, or sleeping, and not much is really going on. These are rare times of respite from going from job to job, you can spend time hunting for criminals, patrolling a crime hot spot area or catching up on some much needed administration. This is quickly destroyed when someone mentions that it is 'Q'... As soon as the Q word is used you can expect a full moon and all the crazies come out to play, cars will crash, domestic incidents will erupt and the illusion of calm and serenity we covet so much is destroyed in seconds.

I'm not saying you should hide from work, quite the opposite, use these times to play catch up and go hunting for burglars. However, don't go looking for trouble where it isn't, in the bad old days we used to drive around with our window open just waiting for someone to call us a name, ' Oi wanker cop', that was enough, out of the car, nose to nose with a group of rowdy youths just waiting to have enough to get a public order offence out of them. This is pointless and all you are doing is failing these young people, yes they need gripping at times and put on the back foot so they know we run the streets and not them. The public order tactic is good for those times and I have used it many times when dealing with neighbourhoods that have high rates of Anti-Social Behaviour. But pick your battles wisely, especially if you are single crewed. When I worked in a city we were usually double crewed and our back up was just around the corner, however, when I was working in a county force, I found I had to adjust my tactics, engaging in a confrontation on your own can go wrong rapidly. One such incident happened to me, I was driving through a village and a drunk outside a Chinese takeaway shouted at me, 'WANKER', so I pulled up and asked him what his problem was? In the cities most people back down and back off knowing that the cavalry will be nearby and they will end up in handcuffs. In the countryside this is not the case, the suspect looked straight at me and repeated his insult and began walking towards me with bad intent. I had no choice but to act and using my car door I slammed it open into him to knock him backwards(sect 3 CLA) as he went backwards I drew and delivered a shot from my incapacitant spray, which had very little effect on him. I then had to fight this person on the floor to get him into handcuffs and arrest him for a public order offence. I had called for 'assistance' on my personal radio and it was coming... my back up finally arrived 15 minutes later, DON'T BITE OFF MORE THAN YOU CAN CHEW. If you do have to withdraw, then do so with dignity, let the dust settle, and then go back later mob handed and deliver the required justice, I mean positive outcome.

Overtime, handovers and sticking in till the job is done

When you sign up to be a Police Officer you also sign up to a chaotic and unpredictable life, let's be honest, that's why you joined. You want the thrill of the chase, the action, the adrenaline of taking down a bad guy, being a hero, or you want to be involved in complex and interesting cases where you safeguard a child or victim of a sex crime. Whatever you joined for, it doesn't often get done in an 8 hour shift, it often involves early starts, late finishes and unhappy partners at home.

'Sticking in' is the true sign of a committed Officer, you started something and you want to take it to completion. This is a good option for the investigation as the OIC(Officer in case) will have a full understanding of the case and the various dynamics that are in play, such as, associations between victim and suspect that may help prove vulnerability, or the OIC has taken on the job as a personal project which will lead to a quality prosecution. As someone who often 'stuck in', I was frustrated when I handed a good prisoner over to another crew on the next shift. They didn't have the same commitment or buy in to the case, they were mostly pissed off because they had been given a handover and that meant they were unable to do their own work that they had been planning to do that day. In cases like this you would come back on duty to find your suspect had been released 'under investigation' or 'bailed' back to you with only a cursory interview completed. This would mean that the investigation had stalled, the suspect released, the victim scared and dissatisfied, and you would now have to play catch up to keep the victim engaged and get the suspect charged.

In some cases you have no choice but to hand over your prisoner; there may be no overtime available, you are coming off a night shift, or your investigation requires the skills of specialist investigators in sexual offences, high risk domestic violence or serious assaults. Don't be disheartened at these handovers, it's not your doing, it's policy and the correct people are going to complete whatever you started. With that in mind you must make sure that the new investigators have everything possible to drive forward the investigation. Complete a 'Handover proforma' if that is something your force has, if not, invent one, you will be hailed as a hero.

Detail everything you have done,

- Incident number/ crime number/ Date & Time of incident.
- Full circumstances of the investigation.
- Names of victims/witnesses/ suspects.
- Statements from everyone involved including your arrest statement, if there are any missing state why and when they can be completed.
- Complete any searches of property and vehicles that you can realistically do, if you can't do them, detail in the report why you didn't do them and give a possible solution to this. Any search records must be exhibited and booked in to property.

- Scene logs exhibited and booked in to property.
- Exhibits, these need to be detailed and booked in to property correctly, all exhibit labels signed and continuity detailed in a statement.
- CCTV, to be treated as an exhibit and booked in to property, if you can, get screen print offs and make a working copy for the new OIC. If you have an establishment like a fast food shop that often aggravates investigations as they say they don't know how to use the CCTV, then seize the whole system and get it downloaded by high tech investigators. The shop will soon learn how to download the content if you do this, often cops walk away and the CCTV is lost or there are delays in getting the footage. If all else fails use your body camera to record it off their shop monitor.
- Detail what scenes of crime work has been completed, if there is a scene preservation still ongoing, ensure the new OIC has an incident number to refer to and they are aware that officers will need replacing. Tag the incident so that SOCO (Scenes Of Crime Officers) attend when they arrive on duty. In cases of serious crime you may be able to contact an out of hours SOCO for advice or they may come in early to deal with the incident.
- Seized vehicles, tag SOCO on the incident and ensure they are aware, ensure you leave details of where the vehicle is for the OIC.
- Welfare, you may have officers deployed to Hospitals on a bed watch with a suspect, or they may be doing a constant observations on a suicidal detainee. They may even be deployed to a crime scene to protect evidence. Make sure that these people are relieved by the oncoming shift as soon as practicable.
- Consider any community impact that may be of note, you may have arrested a child rapist and there is heightened community tensions. The local neighbourhood team will need to jump on this ASAP and they will thank you for an early heads up so they can put safeguards in place with partner agencies.
- Any other details you think will help the investigators; this will include your off duty contact details in case they have an urgent question.

When you start compiling all this stuff you will have to either be dogmatic or enrol the services of a supervisor. Some officers will disappear and leave you to it, they won't want to get involved in the exhibits and they will at all costs avoid having to write a statement. So pester and bully everyone until you get all the information you need to hand over to the investigators that will inherit ' your job'.

Yes, this will still be known as 'your job', and you will be judged on it's quality. Nobody likes to inherit work from other officers, especially if it is of low quality. Would you accept what you are handing over? If not, then get working on it until it is of a decent standard. This is at times beyond your control and you may just handover a prisoner with your arrest statement. Just make sure you leave a reason for this recorded somewhere, I have seen poor handover prisoners quickly interviewed and let loose for the original officer to carry on the investigation. It is an insult to handover poor quality and you wouldn't like it done to you , so don't do it to others. This also forms part of your reputation management, if you constantly handover poor quality work, you will get a name for it and people will not want to work with you, you will be known as lazy and incompetent. If however you are known as someone who 'Sticks In' or produces a quality handover, you will be rewarded with opportunities on specialist departments and promotion.

Overtime

You will be expected to work overtime on a frequent basis, so prepare yourself and your families for this eventuality, however, you should be correctly rewarded for doing this. In the United Kingdom the first half hour of overtime is given to the 'Crown' for free, you will be expected to work this to finish off any bits and pieces before you leave for the day. This does start to grate on you when it feels like you are doing it every day, it is especially unfair when some forces use a term known as 'claw back', this is to adjust your shift hours to fit shifts, sometimes you end up owing the job half hour here and there to compensate for shift alignments. I hated this and seeing them take those half hours from your leave entitlement really pissed me off, the bean counters wouldn't just write it off, they wanted their numbers to be correct, even at the cost of staff morale. To counter this I began to claim my half hours for the crown as TOIL (Time Of In Lieu). This is where you don't get paid for the time you work; you receive time off instead. This countered the claw back and at least I gained something for those half hours.

Paid overtime is the best overtime, and you must make sure you get paid. Any senior officer who tells you that they don't have a budget for overtime is lying, what they are actually trying to do is underspend on their budget to look good to their boss. Yes, there are budgets but they are often blown out of the water due to under staffing and over demand. The Police is not a profit making business, it needs it's officers at all times of the day to protect the public and enforce the law. So don't worry about budgets, stand your ground and ask if there is payment, if there is not then complete a handover and let the next team deal with what you have. The supervisor of the next shift will probably authorise the overtime if yours hasn't got the willingness to do it. If you work over a certain amount of hours you may also be entitled to claim for food, don't feel guilty, you are entitled to this. There are senior officers out there using company credit cards to pay for all sorts, do you think they care about you buying a sandwich when you are working overtime?

Remember, ' **NO PAY, NO PLAY'**, some supervisors will abuse your naivety and willingness to please as a new officer... don't let that be you.

For further reading on this contact the Police Federation, they will have a full list of what you are entitled to.

The Great Unwashed

The British public are a funny bunch, I'm sure it's pretty much the same across the world too, and that's probably why policing people is the same challenge across the world whichever country you live in. Throughout your career you will become used to being let down by the Public, on the whole most are decent hardworking folks who fully support the Police. That is until you have to tell them 'no' and refuse to become their personal tool of vengeance on a neighbour, or until you arrest one of their family. At that point they become selfish, entitled and they lose all traces of reasonableness. You could have been attending a domestic incident where a victim has been battered by their partner, as you are arresting their violent partner the victim will turn on you and you may find a kitchen knife in your back as they're screaming "Don't arrest him, I fucking love him." *Point of note to the uninitiated, never conduct interviews or arrests in the kitchen, its full of sharp weapons and hot liquids that can cause you harm.*

In this chapter I am going to explore some of the characters I have met over the years. I'm pretty sure it won't be long until you meet them too if you haven't already. I will start with a trigger warning; it is not my intention to offend anyone on the diversity/ victim scale, I am talking about my lived experience of people and how they behave.

- **Day to day service users.**

In your service you will come in contact with an array of people from all different backgrounds, some rich, some poor, some caring, some evil. Most 'normal' Citizens only come into contact with the Police if they are a victim of crime, the rest of the time they are busy running their families and going to work. Leave these folks alone to live their lives, if anything consider them as your flock and you are the sheepdog that protects them from the wolves, patrol their streets to keep their homes safe whilst they're at work or sleeping safely in their beds. These are the people you will have the most in common with, working/ middle class and either in full time employment or retired. Don't unnecessarily target these people by stopping them when they are driving to work or going about their business, use your discretion and if you do find a bald tyre or see them commit a minor traffic offence, give them words of advice, a prosecution does nothing but destroy hearts and minds within the demographic that supports the Police the most. The same goes for the kids in this demographic, you will see them walking around in clean fashionable clothes, floppy haircuts and they lack the scowl or attitude of a street wise kid, they're more like the kids from the Inbetweeners TV show. Pointlessly targeting these kids, as with any youths, is an act that can have an effect on the rest of their lives and their attitudes towards law enforcement, so be firm and fair with them but make best use of your discretion and avoid prosecution, but, in some cases you will have no choice and will have to deal with them robustly if they escalate.

Even in this working/middle class demographic you will encounter some bizarre people who live in a nice area but fail to maintain their own personal hygiene and their homes are left in disrepair and unclean, there is no clear line, no black and white, just shades of grey. As an example of this I once went to a report of a burglary at a pub, the thieves had broken into the flat above the pub whilst the landlord was downstairs serving customers. When I walked into the flat, the whole place looked like it had been ransacked; clothes hanging out of drawers and strewn across the floor, broken furniture, it even looked like they had purposely emptied the bins out in each room too. I commented on the state of the flat, " WOW, THEY'VE REALLY GONE TO TOWN HERE, MESSED THE PLACE RIGHT UP," what we call an untidy search. The landlord, who was only in his mid-twenties looked at me with an embarrassed grimace on his face and admitted that this was how he and his partner actually lived and the burglars hadn't caused any of the mess! I'm still not sure who was more embarrassed, him or me?

On the other side of the scale you will encounter some people whose existence surprises you that they have made it to adulthood alive; they can't hold down a job, they smell unclean, they are poorly educated, they've been in jail . For whatever reason in life they have taken a different path, it could have been that they were born into a criminal family or they have fallen from grace and now live a life of addiction to whatever drug they chose, be that alcohol or illegal substances like crack and heroin. Do not be too quick to look down your nose at them, you may have been bought up in the afore mentioned working/ middle class background and had the benefit of a college or university education; but these people have had a different education, they have survived a life time of abuse and neglect and they know the streets you are trying to Police like the back of their hands. They have criminal experience and crime is how they make their living, they do not feel guilty for lying to you, you are just an occupational hazard to them, they have seen hundreds of wet behind the ears cops coming and going since they were small kids watching their parents being arrested. It is a good idea to show empathy in your dealings but these individuals will run rings around you if you let them. Be firm and fair and don't be too trusting and avoid being dragged into their world too much, your empathy shouldn't turn to sympathy and you definitely shouldn't inherit their problems, sign post them to the correct services and leave it in their hands to save themselves. If you do get too involved it can have an effect on your own mental wellbeing and may lead to inappropriate relationships and corruption.

"DO NOT TRY TO RESCUE SOMEONE WHO DOES NOT WANT TO BE RESCUED, AND BE VERY CAREFUL ABOUT RESCUING SOMEONE WHO DOES" Jordan Peterson.

- **Complainers and Callers of note.**

These are the individuals who utilise the Police and other emergency services as their own personal parent, bodyguard and friend to keep them company when they are lonely. Every force will have a database of the people who frequently call for the use of their services. A lot of these folks have mental health conditions and they feature on frequent caller logs with both the Fire Service and the Ambulance Service too. There calls will be about low level anti-social behaviour, fall outs with other vulnerable people, and at times, things that have nothing to do with the Police whatsoever. Some callers of note are that far gone that they will report serious crimes such as rape that they have reported a number of times before. These have already been investigated and found to be either lacking evidence or in some cases a figment of their imagination. Although they are annoying these people must be treated with sensitivity and compassion, they have suffered some significant trauma that has made them this way. Be guided by your supervisor who may instruct you to create a vulnerable person report rather than start a full investigation, this decision will be rationalised by them utilising information available about previous calls to that address.

- **Mad or bad?**

You will encounter some of the most evil people in society during your service, some have become this way due to mental illness and they have no real concept of empathy or knowledge that they are actually doing something bad. However, there are some people who are just plain evil, they choose to live a life where they take and destroy whatever they want and have no care for the victims of their crimes. These people can be domestic abusers, rapists, drug dealers, gangsters or any other type of criminal you can think of, even going to jail doesn't stop these people from their trail of disaster. They continue to learn more evil and dishonest ways whilst serving time in jail and they thrive in this environment that gives them power over weaker inmates. Don't be fooled into thinking you, as a street cop, can do anything to help these people. The best thing you can do is hunt them down like the wild animals they are and get them convicted and sent to jail. At least if they are in Jail their evil is contained within an environment that minimises the likelihood of innocent noncriminal victims.

- **The real gangsters**

Also known as Organised Crime Group leaders, as a street cop your interactions with real gangsters will be very limited. They will at all costs try not to come up on your radar for something petty, they're beyond that. Their driving licence will be in order and they will have car insurance, their homes will be neat and tidy and there will be no anti-social behaviour near to their homes either, to an outsider they will look like a normal family living on an estate. If they don't live on the streets they operate on they will have a business of some kind to keep a foothold on their territory. Verbal interactions with the Police are brief and only when necessary, you will feel the power they have as you speak with them, they are enigmatic, you can sense their dominance and it can unsettle you. You may encounter them when off duty, whilst shopping with your families for example, they will be polite, possibly address you by your name, just to let you know that they know who you are, it's an act of dominance, polite dominance but it's still a power trip. You will hear their family name thrown around as a threat of vengeance by people who are associated to them, you will also hear it from people who are trying to use their name to gain the upper hand but actually have no link to them whatsoever, communities live in fear of them and don't want to be caught in the cross fire of threats and vengeance that goes with their name. Don't be surprised if victims will not speak to you, they're scared of what will happen when you are not there to protect them. I recall arresting a burglar once who had burgled the home of a gangsters mum, he didn't know, he was just feeding a heroin addiction. When we informed him of who's house he had ransacked he turned as white as a sheet and began to shake in a fit of fear of what would have happened to him, I think this did more to deter him from a life of crime than anything the courts could have done. If these gangsters had had a different start in life and they hadn't been a criminal they would have been a leader of people in another scenario, they say it's a very thin line between cop and criminal.

In the movies they show successful gangsters moving into big mansions and living a movie star life style. In my experience this is not what happens, most stay either on or very near to their power base, the streets they run. This has to happen for a number of reasons, here are a few for you to consider,

1. keep control of their territory, if the cats away the mice will play, and that's the same here. The gangster needs to know what's going on in their neighbourhood as its happening. Is a younger upstart on the estate trying to undermine them or take control of their organisation for example. Also their foot soldiers live on that estate and so do their families. Who is upsetting who? Who has been seen talking to the Police?

2. Safety in numbers, they know the streets, the people and they will know who the local cops are too. They may even control one or two of the local cops who have fallen into a desperate situation and have been corrupted. It has been known for female officers to be targeted by criminals like this, some girls like a bad boy and they blindly fall for the charm and lifestyle on offer. It's the same for male cops too, they may meet them at the gym and build a relationship, steroids get involved, a few quiet conversations and invites to social events are made, it's a pathway to corruption and this always ends badly, mostly for the cop who is just being used to access information.

3. Protection, As I have already said in the safety in numbers paragraph, they are protected in their enclave, there will be no witnesses to any crimes they commit and people will shelter and hide them from the law if required.

Real gangsters can be of use if you cultivate them effectively. I say this in a very guarded way as these people are masters at manipulation and control, they lack any empathy and they can turn to violence at the drop of a hat. The gangster doesn't want the Police anywhere near his home or his business, they are well known for owning cash businesses such as gyms, scrap yards and pubs, historically they have used these to launder money through but this has been tightened up in recent years, but they still gravitate to this kind of trade. So, if Police enforcement operations are frequently in their eye line they will feel unsettled and nervous that the cops will stumble over their criminal activity. If you detain one of their soldiers in a stolen car, stop search a runner with a kilo of drugs then the risk to them escalates dramatically when there is Police activity in their area. When this happens you can turn it to your advantage, the gangster will do whatever they have to do to survive, this includes becoming an informant. I recall being part of a proactive team that was chasing down a well-known Burglar who had been targeting victims at night, stealing the car keys from their homes or threatening them in the street with weapons in an act of Robbery. We pulled out all the stops for this guy, proactive patrols, intelligence gathering, surveillance teams etc. This constant attention on the estate was not welcome for those going about their daily lives, car chases put their children at risk, helicopters buzzing around at night disturbed their peace. It also pissed off and unsettled the real gangsters who ran the estate. I knew this and I decided to make an approach on one such individual, there was no great plan about it, I just walked up to him in the street and said words to the effect of

"Hello mate, you don't know me, you're Mr X, I know you're quite connected around here, I bet you hate all these cops being around here?"

He stood there not letting any emotion out.

" I can tell you why all this activity is happening, and you can stop us from being here, we are looking for XXX, he's causing grief for you and everyone else, once we have him we can back off."

Within a couple of days we had received anonymous tip offs of the location of the suspect and he was detained soon afterwards.

I'm not saying that you have to get into bed with these people, but I am saying that they can be of use if you know what you are doing and willing to take a step into the lost art of Police Officers talking to people.

- **Travellers,**

I have to say that most travellers are normal folks just getting on with their lives, they run businesses and work with horses, they don't want to be involved in crime, however, elements within the travelling community have become one of the largest Organised Crime Groups (OCG) in the UK. This does suggest that they are organised, they're not, they just have a common culture and a network of contacts across the country. This network makes hunting down someone who is wanted for a criminal offence quite challenging, they could have been literally anywhere in the country, most who are on the run usually get caught in the act of committing an offence or during a Police vehicle pursuit where the suspect crashes and is identified through fingerprints or DNA after giving false details in custody.

Travellers usually live on either council run sites or privately owned camps that only let family and close friends live on them, in some communities they have been known to park on the road outside family houses and the street is turned into a makeshift site, with power cables leading from the nearby houses to their trailers. Some sites are friendlier than others, you will feel the mood when you arrive, you may be welcomed and offered tea. I have chased suspects onto sites before and the residents have actually helped to detain the suspect, especially if they have driven dangerously on the site and scared their kids, or you may be met with aggression and become baited into being distracted and when you're not looking your police car windows are smashed in.

You rarely see the old type of traveller that continually moves around on a permanent basis, living like this is arduous work and some families choose to do this only in the summer. But when these guys arrive on a sports field near you, you will soon know about it, every resident in that area will be up in arms about the mess that is being left behind and the rise in petty crime and anti-social behaviour. There is nothing stopping you as a Police officer from speaking with the travellers who have landed, in fact you are encouraged to do so, find out how long they plan to stay for example. The Police will be asked to assist in serving notices on travellers that are either on private land or public open spaces. The travellers will know the law better than you do and will usually move on before an official eviction, but make sure your knowledge of legislation is up to date or they will run rings around you.

If the weather is bad they will look for a hard standing to camp on due to the wet conditions, and they will be wanting to stay put until the ground dries up enough for their trailers not to sink in the mud. This may be a perfect time to show some empathy, consider if you would have liked to have been on the road in poor weather conditions with nowhere to park without everything sinking in the mud. Some supermarkets allow short term visits on their carparks for a few days and they allow the use of their toilets as long as there is no anti-social behaviour or theft in the store.

Be prepared for the children, they will see you coming and make a beeline for you, they'll mess with your car, your belt kit, your hat and your mind. They will barrage you with a hundred questions and they will not leave you alone until one of the parents tells them to.

You may encounter a trailer/caravan that has been abandoned and set fire to, this is usually done when the owner has died. It is believed unlucky to keep the trailer for someone else to use, I'd imagine this was initially done as part of disease control.

Criminal behaviour within the traveller community is not too dissimilar to that of an average housing estate. Some are petty criminals who target shops and steal metal off the rail networks and diesel from farms. But you also have your more serious criminal groups who are very inventive and adaptable, they can be targeting elderly people for their money by pretending to be from the water board one day, and then the next day they can be dragging a cash point out of a wall with a piece of stolen plant machinery.

Violence in the traveller community is also similar to any other community, but it does differ in some respects too.

Pub Fights, gangs of male travellers can descend onto a pub which causes quite a bit of concern to landlords and customers alike, you would have the same reaction if a large group of drunken football fans arrived in your local pub whilst you were relaxing with your family. The days of signs on doors saying 'NO TRAVELLERS' are long gone and any pub that does that can expect to be sued in court. What usually happens when a gang of men turn up is that they drink heavily and become very boisterous and loud very quick. Now travellers have suffered years of discrimination and hatred in this country, some have earnt a poor reputation and others have not. But what this causes is a siege mentality, everyone hates us, so we are going to hate everyone back and then some! This hypersensitivity, mixed with alcohol, drugs and a mob mentality makes those situations a tinder box that are waiting for the spark to set it off. Eventually someone will say something or a take a sideways look at the wrong person and it erupts into disproportionate violence that often leads to serious assault injuries. It takes a brave landlord to step in and eject these gangs so don't be surprised if you get the call to help them.

Domestic and honour based violence. This is a crime that is often hidden in the traveller community and it is very rare for you to receive a report of this nature. Children in the travelling community leave school very young and therefore they do not have the social interaction that we are used to with people outside of our families and communities. This does enable a very insular life where they can keep their traditions alive, both good and bad. Things you may encounter are arranged and forced marriages, domestic violence, honour beatings for bringing the families name into disrepute and child neglect/abuse too. These crimes are prevalent in many communities, but the risks are magnified in insular communities where the victim has no one to turn too. Therefore, if you are approached by a victim in a case like this you must elevate it to the highest of risk factors and get them into safe accommodation asap.

Their abusers will be making proactive efforts to find them and bring them back to the situation they have fled from.

In fighting, believe it or not, travellers are not all friendly chuckling lads, with a cheeky accent, that have the crack together and live like a band of brothers. You will encounter feuds between families that have been fought for years. Some of these feuds are played out on Video Hosting Social Media sites like You tube. One of the parties will be offering to fight someone from another family and they'll tell the world why it's happening. The video aspect is used due to the lack of reading and writing skills within some of the groups involved. The subsequent violence is extreme and merciless, some duke it out in a straightener one on one, and some ambush their prey and inflict significant life changing injuries on them, I recall one traveller being sliced with a Stanley knife from the top of his spine to his anus in a savage revenge attack.

- **Football Hooligans.**

Football fans come into a number of categories; You have the family who want to cheer on their local team and enjoy the game, you have the old guys who have always supported the team and just want to get out and enjoy their day, and then You have what is called the 'HARD CORE' and the 'FRINGE' groups.

The 'Hard Core' are also broken into groups; you have the old and bald who are usually in their 40's and 50's, they are the leftovers from the football terrace violence of the 1980's and 1990's, they usually look like a battered bulldog with no hair and have a standard uniform of branded clothing like Henry Lloyd, Ben Sherman or Stone Island. They stand in the centre of the crowd like generals with their minions around them all with their arms outstretched with a 'come on' attitude as they taunt the opposing fans. They chant and egg on the younger hard core (youth element) to start trouble, the younger hard core dress in a similar way but with a more up to date look. They look healthy and childlike; they are called by names such as the 'baby squad,' in times of war these lads would be our Infantry and football grounds can hold over 32000 fans of a similar age, large armies can be built if we need them. But on the football terraces these baby soldiers will do as they are told by their generals and often get used as cannon fodder to prevent the generals from getting into any actual fighting, some things are the same in all armies.

The 'Fringe' groups are usually working lads who are out with their mates and have no real affiliation to the organised groups. They want to be seen with the Hard Core but only want to be half in and not fully commit to organised violence, they get pissed up and make a lot of noise but when faced with a PSU of officers and the prospect of a night in the cells they usually disappear at the first opportunity.

Most football hooligans don't want to fight! They will get pissed up and damage cars whilst dancing on them, throw glasses in a pub and get all aggressive with their arms stretched out shouting "c'mon you want some," as soon as the police run at them they usually turn tail and run, It's part of their game... Like I said they usually run, not always though, so be prepared to get hands on if the situation escalates. And remember these are young fit men of military fighting age, do you consider yourself fit enough, or skilled enough to tackle these people? If not, make a plan, get fit, learn some practical unarmed defence techniques beyond that of your basic training, get used to dealing with violence.

- **Community Leaders**.

At some point you will get an attachment to a neighbourhood team, this is where you will learn the skills of a beat officer whose primary role is community policing. These neighbourhood officers are usually more mature and have quite a few years' experience, so make sure you listen to them and take away anything positive you can from your interactions.

Part of your attachment will include meeting local community leaders, these can include,

1. Religious Leaders
2. Political Leaders
3. Neighbourhood Watch
4. Youth Leaders & Self-appointed street leaders

Meeting these good folks can leave you with that warm community feeling, that glow you get when you interact with nice people, you feel you are making a difference and listening to the needs of the community. However, not all of these people are your friend,

Religious leaders will say nice things and talk about peace between different groups. They may be useful when there is unrest, an Iman for example, calling for gangs of youths to go home to their parents and to stop rioting. They can also feedback how some of their community are feeling after a recent event such as a murder and warn of any potential disorders. Just be aware that they do not speak for everyone who follows their religion, just because someone professes to follow a certain faith it doesnt mean that they're not a criminal too, and they can use their faith as a cover or to intimidate others in their community.

Political Leaders, well what can I say, one minute they're a school crossing lady and the next minute they're your local councillor... Standards vary. You have professional politicians who are parachuted in from the home counties, to a safe seat, to represent one of the major parties as a member of parliament (MP). They're well educated and from a middle to upper class background, they know how to schmooze their way through the corridors of power and how to lie to their constituents so convincingly they keep getting voted in every 4 years. These are the people who members of the public write to when they have a problem with the standard of service they receive from the Police. The MP will receive the letter of complaint, then request a meeting with the local Inspector or the Chief Constable and try to find out what actually happened. What has usually happened is that the member of public had too high expectations or were in the wrong themselves. The MP must then reply to the member of the public and try to appease them by stating they have addressed the issue with the Chief Constable. You don't have much to fear from these people unless you're getting in the way of their political career.

You are more likely to have dealings with locally elected officials who work for parishes and wards, these are the afore mentioned school crossing ladies, or they may be retired folks or local business owners with time on their hands. Mostly good people, but some do have political agendas and some crave power over their communities. A lot of normal people avoid local politics due to the types who get involved, petty power struggles break out and egos get in the way of true progress. These individuals can be a real pain in the arse and you have to interact with them due to their 'elected ' status. What they can be useful for is funding, I utilised one of my local parish councils to fund Police Bicycles for the rural Police Office that I was running at that time, they were more than happy to fund the bikes and other schemes I had in the pipeline too. Use them when you can but be aware that they are politically aligned, but lack the professionalism of the MP, so they may cause you grief by over complaining on behalf of their Parish.

One final point about Politicians, there have been many news stories about corruption in politics, this happens at all levels. It may be an MP taking cash for questions in the houses of parliament, or it may be a Parish councillor taking back handers for contracts or embezzling funds. Investigations of this nature will usually go to the Economic Crime Unit or one of the Serious Crime Departments. Keep a professional distance from all politicians, power corrupts, and they may have intentionally spun you into their web of crimes as a layer of protection, they will take people down with them when they're finally caught.

Neighbourhood Watch, if you have never watched the film 'Hot Fuzz,' which is a comedy film about Police life in a small town, I suggest you do. This film not only has a very accurate account of some of the Police characters you will meet in your career, but it also shows the extremes of some neighbourhood watch types. You will find that most of their ranks are retired well-meaning folks who want to make a difference and contribute to their community, you will also get the 'Political' characters from the Parish councils too. They hate the thought of crime and disorder on their streets and set out to make their area a 'no go' area for criminality. They can be quite effective, and they're great if you want leaflet drops doing or if you want volunteers to work on a crime prevention stand at a local event. I've even used them to help with property marking and smart water initiatives. Although the majority are great folks who fully support the Police, you have to identify and manage those who begin to have mission creep. They start off targeting criminals, they then realise that they actually live in a nice area and there's actually not that much crime, they then start looking for problems. These problems can range from kids riding bikes on pavements, bikes with no bell to warn others and youths hanging around on parks, how dare they hang around on a park? It becomes comical at first, but then it escalates and causes division in the community between young and old, this lack of tolerance becomes the focus of their efforts and they will pester the local commander or even the chief constable about it. Then the local beat team gets tasked with dealing with it and a disproportionate amount of time and resources are spent on trivial matters.

Youth Leaders & Self-appointed street leaders

Youth leaders are great and they come from a multitude of backgrounds, they can be people who organise sporting events such as football and boxing, or they can set up organised events for the local youths to attend as a distraction from crime and drugs. These people can be useful to task to visit areas of high anti-social behaviour, they can talk to the kids on a different level than the Police in uniform ever can.

The ones to be aware of are the self-appointed street leaders, I'm all for giving people a second chance and letting them give back to the communities from they have offended against, but I am always very wary of the 'ex criminal,' 'ex drug dealer' types who profess themselves to be the local street saviour of the youth in their community. Some have genuinely grown up and seen that their ways were wrong and they want to help the kids, however, some are doing this with an agenda. They are anti Police, very political and looking for reasons to complain about any Police action, they have become social justice warriors and they will not engage with the Police in any reasonable dialog and they reinforce a them and us culture.

- **Media.**

The media are a double edged sword, as a street cop you don't really have that much to fear from them unless you are doing something horrendously wrong. Social media however is a different creature all together, I'm sure most of you will have seen the endless reels or short clips of cops being made to look stupid by a vlogger or social justice warrior armed with a phone camera.

One thing both of these creatures have in common though is the need for content. That may be videos, quotes, column inches in a newspaper, they all want to fill their publications and sell their creation to gain financial reward from advertising and monetisation. Sensationalised headlines act as 'click bait' and readers delve into an article about a cop only to find they are bombarded by adverts and a milk toast article which has no resemblance to the headline.

Local News agencies can be your friend, they want the afore mentioned content and they especially like crime stories. So, if there is an initiative to tackle street robberies or car theft going on, include the local media, build it in as part of your media strategy when planning the operation, take them with you when you execute a warrant, live action video footage of a Police raid makes great news. The news agencies will get their content, your operation will get exposure and the public will be informed, everyone's a winner. Unless it's a story they cannot avoid the local press will not actively pursue the Police in a negative light, it is in their interest to keep this working relationship as friendly and reciprocal as they can.

If you get the chance to attend a media training session, then do it, you will learn about how the media machine works, what things to avoid saying and how to construct a press release. I had a good working relationship with our Corporate Communications team (AKA Press Office) and I often sent them press releases about good police work and initiatives in the local area, I have also had good relationships with individual reporters who championed our cause and highlighted the great work we were doing.

Do not be afraid of the press when you are out and about, if they ask you a question and you are not confident to answer them, you can direct them to your supervisor or if you are alone you can direct them to Corporate Communications, real reporters will respect this and they won't hound you or try and belittle you. This type of behaviour comes from the Social media vloggers who are just after sensationalist exposures and likes on their page for monetised returns. I know it is of little comfort when you or your colleagues have gone viral on the internet because an incident has escalated out of control or because someone looks unprofessional. You will be able to see the difference between the real reporters and the internet trolls. The best way to survive these trolls is to look back at some of the advice you have received in training, from your tutor and from books like this one. Know your powers, use them with confidence, wear your uniform with pride, that includes wearing your hat. You won't believe the difference wearing your hat can have on public perception, you may feel silly in it but it's a statement of professionalism and looks so much better. My pet hate is watching the news and seeing overweight scruffy cops with their hands in their pockets whilst talking to potentially dangerous criminals or stood guarding a crime scene.

The time to fear the media is when you are in the wrong, you can't be held accountable for policy decisions from your chief constable, nor can you take the blame for other officers who hit the national headlines when they are exposed as corrupt or sexual predators, the only thing you have to answer for is your actions. In a time where everyone carries a camera, even the police, you have to be so much more aware of perceptions and how you say things and the way they can be interpreted. But like I said you have body cameras now too, these are great for destroying any allegations that are made against you, or of only part of a video clip is shown that shows you in a bad light. Your unedited body camera footage can be used to great effect to protect you against allegations in these circumstances.

- **Compassion Fatigue**

 On any given day you could encounter all the people listed in this chapter, and again the next day, and on top of that you have been working 24/7 shifts. Eventually this takes its toll and you begin to see the world very differently, you become sceptical and doubt everyone's honesty. People will talk to you when off duty and straight away you will become defensive, you will judge them in seconds by the way they speak, the way they dress and the slightest hint that they are a threat to your inner peace will lead you to pre judge them and dismiss them from your life. This needs to be managed as it can have a significant effect on your personal life and the personal lives of your family. It is easy to become institutionalised and surround yourself with Police friends but take time to think back to life before the Police. You will have to allow people into your life and pull the barriers down sometimes or you will live a paranoid and lonely life.

(Authors note: Still don't trust anyone unless you know them 100%, then still be careful.)

Snitches, liars and intelligence gathering.

Information and intelligence is the life blood of the Police service, without it we are a ship without a rudder that drifts aimlessly until it crashes on the rocks and sinks. So, every opportunity to feed the machine must be taken. By now I hope you have understood how important it is to know your area and to know who is a threat to you and the community. Intelligence comes in many forms and from many different sources, it may be raw human intelligence from a source or community contact. Or it can be gained through lawful use of the internet and open source searches that identify an offender at the scene of a crime. But as a police Officer on patrol you will see and encounter things that you believe will be of intelligence value on a daily basis. Look for the absence of normal, question everything you see, why are there no drug dealers on a corner you know is usually busy, is there a turf war about to start? Why has one of the local criminals got a broken arm, has he received a punishment beating, or crashed a stolen car?

Start feeling comfortable in speaking with people, learn some conversation starters, don't always go in hard and start interrogating people like they're suspects, learn the soft skills. Learn about the commodities that make your community what it is, is it Heroin, Cocaine, Cannabis, MDMA or is it one of the more exotic mix of chemicals that destroys lives and communities? If you know your commodities, you will know what to look for, smell for and you will see behaviours or signs of those drugs being used. Talk to drug users and their families about the local drug scene, the cost, the weights, the availability of such things too, they may even tell you who the local dealers are.

Get out of your cars and start talking to gangs of youths, you may break down a few barriers and you may be able to build an intelligence picture of who is associating with who. Talk to the lonely old people when you get a chance, they see and hear everything and are usually invisible to most people, they often put the kettle on too.

Always consider why someone is telling you something, humans will naturally do what is best for them and their motivations will usually be one of the following reasons,

- Revenge, a spurned lover, a hatred for someone.

- Self-preservation, criminals often do more harm to other criminals than they do to general members of the public. A criminal may also inform on their associates to lessen a prison sentence, this is done covertly and a letter or 'text' as it is known is handed to the judge before sentencing.

- Protection of a family member or close associate. A parent for example, who sees what their child is getting involved in, parents see and hear everything and are, like old people, thought of as invisible.

- Financial gain, a paid informant or Covert Human Intelligence Source (CHIS). Their motivation is not always greed, it may form any of the other reasons listed but the financial gain is a bonus for them. I have known parents who were CHIS take the money to pay for their kids school uniforms and shoes, this is not greed, it is a level of survival many people in the Police do not understand.

- A sense of injustice, they have been wronged, they were a victim of crime, maybe the police did their best and the source wants to help them with other matters as they're sick of the crime in their community.

- Rid themselves of competition, a drug dealer perhaps.

- A strong sense of community responsibility, a lot of information comes from good people in the community, they may run a project or help look after the children of drug users at a centre. Be careful not to over use these people or show them out as sources, they tread a difficult line and need to maintain the trust of those they service.

- Theological differences within a community and the hatred of radicalisation that promotes terrorism and violence.

I am sure you may be able to name many other reasons why people will inform on each other, but these are a good starting point. When you have gathered this information you will have to consider a few things,

- What to do with it, will you act on it there and then? If you're considering this, always consider the safety of your source. Are they the only person who knows this information, will you acting on it compromise them and put them at risk? Consider why they have given you this information, is it malicious, are they using you to do their dirty work? When dealing with informants always remember that **'The dog wags the tail, the tail doesn't wag the dog,'** You are in control of that situation not them, you are the dog. If you feel like they're starting to give you jobs to do or they are pressuring you to act on the information, cut them loose and submit an intelligence log about your concerns.

- Or will you pass it into the system and let it go through the process of information being turned into intelligence? To do this it will have to be inputted into the force computer system. It will need to be graded as to its quality and its provenance, so if it is listed as anonymous and believed to be malicious for example, it will receive a lower grading.

- If you use the same source of information and record it on the systems more than 3 times in a short period of time, it will trigger a notification and you may be approached to ensure that you are not running a source and tasking them to collect intelligence for you. Tasking of sources is conducted by a Dedicated Source Handling Unit (DSHU), They have to have authorities and safeguards in place to protect the source and the organisation against abuse.

- Always protect your sources and do not tell people on your team who your sources are, they will gossip and there are corrupt officers who will use that information for their own gain. You may end up handing your source over to a CHIS handler from the DSHU, you may not even know it, the CHIS handler may have seen your intelligence report and they may have made an approach and recruited them as a registered source. If this happens take it as a compliment and move on and find another source, they now belong to the DSHU and you will be putting them at risk if you continue to debrief them for intelligence.

What is a CHIS?

A covert human intelligence source (CHIS) is defined as a person who establishes or maintains a personal or other relationship with another person for the covert purpose of facilitating anything that:

i) Covertly uses such a relationship to obtain information or to provide access to any information to another person; or

ii) Covertly discloses information obtained by the use of such a relationship or as a consequence of the existence of such a relationship.

In layman's terms it's an informant.

Debriefing a CHIS

You may on rare occasions get the opportunity to work with the DSHU, if you get the chance grab it with both hands and make the most of it. If you get selected to join them as a permanent team member your world will be opened up to a life of covert policing, deception and tradecraft that will be used to keep you and the source safe. During my time as a Source Handler I developed a method of debriefing sources that kept the meetings on track and ensured the safety and welfare of all involved. I have utilised the mnemonic **CATPRINTS.**

C= Cover story, what is it? Ensure you have a believable story as to why you are together at a specific place. Utilise Tradecraft to ensure that the CHIS and Handlers are not being followed to the meeting.

A= Any welfare issues? You are responsible for the welfare of your CHIS, if their life is a mess they will be less effective. You can help them with some of their problems too, signpost them to their GP, marriage counselling, or any agency that can help them. They will thank you for taking an interest in their welfare and because of that they will reciprocate by working harder for you.

T= Time...do have enough? If either party is in a rush then they need to let it be known, if there is insufficient time, reschedule the meeting.

P= Pay, always pay your sources on time and in full, do this early on in the meeting, this will reinforce that you mean business and that they will get paid for any good intelligence that they are about to give you.

R= Revisit Taskings from last meeting, discuss any tasking you gave during the last meeting, ask for and expect updates on the points you tasked. Remember you are the dog and they are the tail that wags. They are paid for intelligence; you are not their cash point.

I= Intelligence requirement, what do you want them to keep an eye out for, this is not a tasking, you may be asking them if they have access to a certain person, group, location, or product such as stolen property, 'If you hear anything lets us know' conversation. This may then lead onto a tasking at a later date.

N= New Intelligence from CHIS, has the CHIS come across new information that we were not aware of and they were not tasked to get? Ensure they are getting this intelligence holistically and they are not 'self-tasking'.

T= Taskings, this is an authorised request to seek out what new intelligence you want the CHIS to actively seek out.

S= Safe route in and out of the meeting, utilise tradecraft to ensure the CHIS and the Handlers are able to attend meetings in safety.

Handling CHIS is one of the best jobs in the Police Service, it does however come with a lot of responsibility. You are responsible for their safety, some CHIS don't help themselves and can compromise you and put all involved at risk, they will actually tell people that they're talking to the Police. Some will also appreciate your care for them so much that they will want to split their earnings with you! Don't do it, explain to them that you are not allowed and that you would face prosecution and lose your job if someone found out. They may reply that 'no one will know', well just remember they're a CHIS, they inform on people for a living, don't trust them, they will inform on you too!

DEAD OR IN BED

Looking for the missing

Missing persons are going to be part of your daily working life, it will be a very rare day that you won't have at least one person listed as missing on your area. Missing persons or Mispers as they are known come in various categories, here are a few to consider,

High Risk, This will include young children, vulnerable people and people considered as being at risk of suicide or significant harm. A lot of effort is put into locating these people and you may spend the whole shift looking for them, search teams can be employed, national alerts can be put out, especially when children are involved. In instances of high risk missing persons, resources such as helicopters and mobile phone cell site location trackers are put to great use.

Frequent flyers, You will soon get to know the frequent flyers, many are in social care and are lured away from their placement by either family or people that are exploiting them. Do not be surprised to find a frequent flyer is a high risk missing person too, they are usually young, vulnerable and are being sexually exploited or being used for drugs activity such as county lines.

Some just don't like being in care and want to be where they originally came from. Many of these kids are passed around care homes as they become too difficult to handle, they won't settle with families and they eventually end up in a flat of their own or even possibly jail.

Freedom seekers, these people are not missing, they just don't want to be found by the person reporting them missing. That may be because they have reached a point in their life where they've had enough of their partner and just pack a bag and leave, or they could have been in an abusive relationship, a victim of honour based violence or are being subjected to an arranged marriage. In cases like this you can usually locate them and assess them as safe and well. However, you must not report their location back to the people reporting them as missing, if they have left and don't want to be found then you must respect that, you may be placing them in danger if you expose their location. The only information that may be reported back is that they have been located and that they are safe and well. There may be times when a wanted person is listed as a missing person too, they may be on the run from the Police but they are also subject to a threat to life from other criminals, it happens quite frequently, they need to be found to make them aware of the threat and also to make sure they haven't been a victim of the criminals and murdered or seriously injured.

When searching for Mispers the basics are a key element to a successful outcome, attendance at their missing from address is non-negotiable. Details of the Misper need to be taken and a photo of them too for circulation to searching officers and a full search of the address must be completed. This means the whole property! The Mispers bedroom will be a trove of information and intelligence, are there any clothes missing? Have they left a note, do they have a diary? Are there any indicators about their lifestyle such as drug abuse or their mental state? You will also need to search their room to see if they are actually hiding under the bed. This does happen and it is why the first thing you must do is search the whole house, in the loft, under the beds, under the stairs, the garden, the shed etc. There have been many cases where people have faked a disappearance for financial gain or just for the attention of being missing, some of these cases have triggered national searches and campaigns to fund the family of the Misper in an elaborate fraud. When searching you must also look for signs of foul play, the reporting person may be reporting them missing when they have actually been murdered.

An example of the basics working was shown when a foster family reported a missing 3 year old girl who was in their care. She had been safeguarded from abusive parents and the father had historically made threats to find her and snatch her back. The foster family who lived in a very nice rural location had spent the day with the child and their other kids enjoying the sun and playing around the house and garden. The little girl was noticed to be missing and both parents went into panic mode; they made the call to the Police and the balloon went up straight away, high risk status, motorway alerts, helicopters and an army of police officers began to descend on the area around the Mispers address. I became ground commander and immediately assigned officers to attend the home address to take details and to conduct a thorough search of the house and grounds. I dispatched another team to search some open water that was nearby too in case the child had wandered off and fell in the water. On arrival I saw a sea of blue lights and officers diligently searching the area around the house and questioning people in the street, I climbed out of my vehicle and walked towards the distressed family who were visibly shaken and upset for obvious reasons. As I neared I became aware of a car parked outside the home address, I peered into the back window and saw a small child fast asleep in a car seat, I pointed the child out and asked, "is this her"? The shriek of relief from the foster parents was immediate and the realisation that the child was safe brought them to tears as they took her from the child seat. The child had become tired and had climbed into the back of the car to sleep whilst the foster father had been cleaning the car earlier that day. Although it was necessary for the balloon to go up and protocols put in place for a missing child to be executed, this example shows the importance of doing that initial visit and search of the premises.

Escalation of searches

If the risk factors associated to a missing person escalate and a significant threat to life or safety has been identified, a search manager may be called upon to coordinate resources in conjunction with whoever is the ground commander, this is usually the duty inspector, but at busy times this can be delegated down to sergeant and PC level too.

If you contact a search manager they will want a raft of information before they commit to bringing out dedicated and trained search teams, I suggest you get this information at hand before you call them, you may even locate the Misper by going through this check list.

<u>Search managers checklist</u>

- Who/ what are we looking for? (person/vehicle/evidence/weapon)
- Factors placing Misper at high risk.
- Last known location.
- Circumstances of the Police being notified.

<u>Analyse possible scenarios</u>

LOST: Person(s) who are temporarily disorientated and wishes to be found (e.g. Someone who has been out walking in the hills and took a wrong trail, now they do not know where they are)

MISSING: Someone who has control of their actions and has decided upon a course of action.

INFLUENCE OF A THIRD PARTY: Someone missing against their own will (e.g. possible abduction or murder)

MISSING DUE TO ACCIDENT, INJURY OR ILLNESS: Examples of this are someone who is victim of a sudden illness or hit by a vehicle in a hit and run scenario. Have they suffered an injury whilst being out walking? Have they potentially fallen into a ditch or a body of water? Consider contacting hospitals in the area to assess if they have your Misper or any unnamed patients.

SUICIDE: This can be achieved in a number of ways; previous history may indicate how they may attempt this if they have tried before. But consider scenarios such as hanging, tablets, drowning, use of firearms and knives.

Background of Misper

Areas frequented: Consider places such as schools, work and social venues like pubs, restaurants or favourite places to go, maybe the grave of a deceased person they were close to.

Do they have access to a vehicle: Consider doing PNC searches and Automatic Number Plate Recognition systems.

Do they have access to cash/bank cards/ Passport: Make enquiries with the bank to see if they have made any significant withdrawals or purchases such as a train ticket. Has a flight been booked? Is their passport missing?

Have they got access to a mobile phone: Consider cell site analysis to locate it, however, be guarded about calling them on it as they may dispose of the phone or it may escalate you into a crisis negotiation situation. Get supervisory permission that has been risk assessed and agreed to a call being made.

Social media: can anyone view any of their content? Does it indicate a check in somewhere, can it be accessed to check location data? Or has it laid dormant since they were reported missing? Apps such as Snapchat can display a friends location if the Misper has not blocked this feature on the app.

Friends, relatives & associates: Identify as many as you can and contact them, be sensitive but ask them if they know of anything that may identify a motive for the person going missing or where they may be.

Physical and Mental Condition: Medication, what kind of medication is it, when was it last taken, what happens if it's not taken, what are the effects?

Any suggestions of Mental Illness or conditions, Alzheimer's, memory loss after an accident or dangerous conditions that makes them to be a threat to themselves or others. Do they have dual diagnosis with addiction such as a drug habit and depression?

How physically fit are they, do they exercise on a regular basis? Were they out exercising when they went missing, what routes do they take when out walking or running? what are the weather conditions like?

Consider speaking to their GP or hospital if associates have no information.

Areas of risk nearby: Considering the factors above are there any areas within the capabilities of the Misper that they may have travelled too? Consider searching these areas, but if you do search an area make sure you search it properly, get enough resources and don't be afraid to climb through bushes and across streams. Dead Mispers have been found by family and friends in areas that have already been searched by the Police, this is very embarrassing to you as an officer and traumatic to the families who will believe you could have saved their family member had you searched properly.

Ultimately it is a process, you have to keep feeding your decision making process with information and intelligence. Unfortunately the Misper is sometimes found dead, no matter how much effort you have put into the search it is very unlikely that you could have changed this outcome, they were probably dead before you were even called to attend the initial report. There was a saying when I joined the Police relating to missing persons,

THEY'RE EITHER DEAD OR IN BED

This saying is still quite true, if someone is going to kill themselves they'll usually just walk off and do it. A dog walker will find them in the woods and the case will be filed as suicide and a sudden death/Coroner's report will be completed. Some people just don't want to be where someone else thinks they should be, they walk off, find somewhere comfortable and safe, and they just stay there, usually in bed. The aim of this saying is really to depersonalise the process of searching for someone, yes it is a process and that's how it must be dealt with. You follow the trail of actions given to you and repeat them as required, if the Misper is found alive, that's great they were in bed(most are found in bed). If they're found dead, you cannot take it personally, it's not the searching officers fault, that person made a decision to take their own life, or someone else made the decision to kill them, that decision had nothing to do with you personally. It's just part of the process and a fact of life, people die, either naturally or by their own hand, in extreme circumstances it's by the hands of others, but ultimately it's not the Police officers fault and the saying 'DEAD OR IN BED' sums it up with two options that the human brain can rationalise and hopefully recover from.

Property, Paperwork and Police Officers.

The average newly recruited British Police Officer is from a working or middle class family and has had no major upset in their lives beyond a family death through old age or illness, and possibly a divorce between their parents. They will have a good education, most likely a university degree and obviously no criminal background of any concern. Therefore their exposure to the service users that a Police Officer comes in contact with daily is very limited before they join the job. This is not a slight at them as a person, but it is a fact of life, you join young and naïve and think you can change the world, that is exactly the type of people we need. We need the young fit officer with a head full of good intentions and the thirst for action, the officer that will chase a burglar through back gardens and over six foot fences at 3am in the rain. We need people who know what is right and what is wrong, they're as financially solvent as a young person can be, this reduces the risk from bribery and corruption from criminals.

New recruits have to come from stable backgrounds and they have to have a good level of education too, not necessarily a degree, but they should have a good working ability with reading, writing and numeracy . If we didn't recruit from this pool of talent the force may be at risk from characters who make rash decisions, have violent outbursts or are dogged with trauma, addiction and mental health conditions due to an abusive upbringing. The job has enough problems with corruption and discipline already without adding characters from dysfunctional backgrounds where they have had to survive extremes of abusive behaviour and questionable morale guidance.

There are 3 things that will always get you into trouble, **Property, Paperwork and Police Officers**, the last one was always historically written as Police Women, but this isn't always the case, and some of the lads are just as much of a risk to you, so I've been inclusive of them too.

Property

You need to keep a tight grip on anything you take possession of, this may be a member of the public handing in a £20 note they found, or an exhibit from a crime scene. Both are as important as each other and they both need to be secured and booked into the property system and store as soon as you can. I once worked for a Detective Sergeant(DS) who liked to keep all his exhibits under his desk, this was convenient for if we needed something, but it was bad practice. I recall us searching for a murder weapon to take to court and it couldn't be found under the desk, panic set in and we searched every nook and cranny until we realised we had submitted it to the laboratory for testing. Imagine that? A murder weapon kept under a desk; can you imagine the fall out if we hadn't located it? Any officer who loses an exhibit may have to answer some very difficult questions from a judge in court and may face disciplinary action for neglect of duty. The same DS also kept drugs in his desk drawer rather than booking them in, this was a disaster waiting to happen, and one day he pissed off the wrong Police Officer who promptly grassed him up to the Superintendent, the DS was lucky not to face serious disciplinary action for this.

Lost property can cause just as much trouble too, if you're ever approached in the street and a member of the public wants to hand in some found property then make sure you record it in your pocket book, get it booked into property, do not leave it in your stab vest for another day. This could have been part of a sting operation to test your integrity and many Police officers have been caught out pocketing small amounts of cash that they think people won't miss.

Paperwork

Thankfully, a lot of reports and files are now online and kept on secure servers. However, you still need to keep them updated and current, some officers struggle with this and some try to keep all the information in their heads. If you were to die or become very sick, who else knows the information that you had kept in your head? No one, and the loss of this information may lead to a failed investigation.

Keep up to date on your investigations, even if you have nothing to add to the report evidentially you can update that you have spoken to the victim for example. Communication with your victims is key, they understand you are busy, but they want to know they haven't been forgotten.

In times of reduced resources and increased demand you may not get a chance to progress your investigations as you are a slave to the radio, and you are going from job to job collecting more reports that you will not get a chance to investigate either. If this happens and your crime queue(list of reports) becomes unmanageable, ensure that you let your supervisor know. They will be sympathetic to your situation as you can be sure they have been there too, that does not mean they will be able to do much to help you though. You will find the rest of the team/ Station/ Force is in exactly the same position and there is no one to pass your jobs on to. Here is how to take action in this situation,

- Don't panic, don't get overwhelmed, don't go sick and don't take it personally.
- Jobs are like spinning plates, some are glass, some are rubber and some are metal. What this means is that you can afford to drop a few plates, just not the glass ones. If you drop a glass plate it smashes and you can never save it or recover that loss, this may be for example cases like Sexual Assault, Domestic Violence or a stalking case. A rubber plate is a case where the victim is the crown, possession of drugs or a public order matter for example, if you drop those plates and leave them for a while they'll bounce back when you get a chance to do them. Now if you drop a metal plate, it will make a lot of noise but it won't break, this may be a complaint from neighbours who have fallen out over parking, or a shop theft and the shop keeper is always phoning in to complain. The metal plates will make a lot of noise when you drop them but ultimately you can pick them up again when you have dealt with the glass plates first.
- List your jobs in priority and start by adding a generic working sheet to every job acknowledging that you are overwhelmed with work and will be prioritising jobs with the highest levels of Threat, Risk and Harm first.
- Identify quick wins,
  1. Is an investigation out of time for prosecution? If so update it, update the victim if there is one and file it to your supervisor.

2. Is an investigation going nowhere? No identifiable suspects, no cctv, no realistic lines of enquiry? If so write it up to that effect and file it to your supervisor. Do not hang onto these reports just because you feel you owe the victim something. Most will understand your limitations and understand why it was filed, just ensure you communicate empathetically with them and apologise on behalf of the organisation.

3. Are you the right person to be investigating something? Some cases belong with specialist teams and they somehow end up on your investigation queue. If you feel your High Risk domestic case should be with a specialist team then write it up and send it to that department for a review.

4. Run an operation on overtime to clear the back log. Look at your force priorities, they'll usually be something like ' Protecting the vulnerable, preventing crime and bringing people to justice.' You can link this to your afore mentioned glass plates, Domestic Violence, Violent Crime or a series of shop thefts by the same offender can have a disproportionate effect on everyone's workload and they come with risks to the organisation. Approach a supervisor or even you station inspector and discuss running a clear up operation on overtime to clear the back log. Once you have a list of all 'violent crime' for example, Your Inspector will need to bid for overtime and you will need to ask for volunteers to work overtime. You will then need a running log of jobs from everyone's crime queue in your department that fit the criteria that need attention by the officers on overtime, they will come on duty and work their way through the jobs, picking up prisoners or finalising the enquiries as they progress. Bit by bit the crimes will disappear from the investigation queues and officers will start to get some breathing space which will enable them to concentrate on the rubber or metal plates. These operations can save lives and they can save yourself and the organisation a lot of embarrassment if a repeat domestic violence victim is murdered and their previous reports have not been investigated. Operations such as these are frequently under taken, especially towards the end of the financial year when the force wants to use up its overtime budgets.

- Consider regime change, is your supervisor actually looking after you? Or are they unintentionally destroying a team crime report by crime report? Some supervisors are not robust enough nor do they have the grit to make quick and accurate decisions in the interest of anyone except themselves. They are risk averse due to fear of criticism from their bosses and they fear complaints from the public. These are the Sergeants who will not file anything until they have every single piece of information even if that information is not relevant. A good supervisor should be giving you a proportionate investigation plan to conduct. A basic one for a shop theft may be something like,
  1. Take statement from shop owner.
  2. Review CCTV for suspects and circulate images for identification if of sufficient quality.
  3. Manage expectations of the victim as to likely outcome if no suspects are identified.
  4. Review intelligence systems for similar incidents with identifiable suspects.
  5. Submit for filing if no suspect identified.

  If your Sergeant or supervisor is continually sending you off on fools errands for multiple statements or unrealistic house to house enquiries then they are failing you. They may just be an acting Sergeant who wants to make a good impression with increased positive outcomes. People like this rarely impress as it is soon noted that their teams investigations are stalled and there is an increased amount of sickness due to stress. However some Sergeants are just built this way and they cannot help but micro manage and over task their officers. If this becomes the norm and you see the ship sinking around you, it is your duty to do something about it, tell the sergeant, if they don't listen, tell the Inspector, this is not snitching, it is survival and Sergeants and supervisors like this are the cause of a lot of stress and sickness.

- Make a start, you will not clear your back log by bitching about the system for hours in the canteen, nor will you achieve anything by going sick. If you go sick there is a good chance your jobs will be waiting for you to return to work, if they have been reallocated you will inherit them back from a grumpy cop that has had to do your work in your absence. Prioritise your work with the glass plates as your first actions and get on with it.

  You have to make a start; however big the challenge is.
  "How do you eat an elephant?... One bite at a time."

Police Officers

If anyone is going to throw you under the bus it won't be a criminal, nor will it be a member of the public, as in real life, your biggest betrayals will come from the people closest to you, and that means you will be at some point in your career stitched up by someone within the organisation. As a shift Sergeant just before retirement I had a queue of Officers just dying to grass on each other, I'd have my daily visit from 'The snitch' telling me that they didn't like the way such and such did this or that, it was truly like being a primary school teacher looking after needy children. Now don't get me wrong, if someone is corrupt or out of line they must be dealt with, and without people telling you what's going on how are you meant to know? But there has to be a degree of balance between malicious complaining and genuine concerns for professional standards. This kind of behaviour was rare in my earlier career, if someone were out of order they'd be told face to face, or a team meeting was called, without supervision present, and the offender was challenged to their face, especially if they had been telling tales.

Maybe this has become more prevalent due to the reduction of officer numbers, which also means the reduction of opportunities for development and promotion too. Someone wants to look good and the only way they can do this is to make someone else look bad. This is a risky strategy and not one I will suggest as a way to career progression. As I have said reputations stay with people for a long time in the Police and if You're known as someone who isn't a team player it will follow you around for the rest of your career.

One of the worst things that I have encountered is officers who are not that proactive and unwilling to get stuck into a disorder or violent arrest criticising those who do. The Police is a violent job and without the people who are willing to get stuck the service will be walked all over by the thugs of society. To my dismay I often saw a gaggle of the snitches crowded around a computer monitor dissecting body camera or CCTV footage of an incident, they were stage by stage picking through the bones of how the other Police Officer was performing, just like internet trolls they were not taking into account the behaviours of the suspect and they didn't have a full understanding of the situation from just a snap shot of video. Every time I saw this I challenged it by openly calling these people out and remind them that last week the same people were criticising their body camera footage, it really angered me that they were so keen to see a colleague fall from grace and be criticised for doing the best they can in any given scenario. Be aware of criticising colleagues in a situation that you were not involved in, you were not the person who had to make that decision at that time and in those circumstances, hindsight is a great thing when you're sat in a comfortable office watching snapshots of video. It is however unhelpful when you are the officer out on the streets facing down a violent criminal.

As a flip side to this, do not expect to have the indefensible defended either. If you have abused your powers or acted in a criminal way you can expect no quarter from your colleagues, the days of officers closing ranks and lying for each other are long gone in a time before even I joined the Police. This closing ranks is not something I have ever seen, you may receive supervisory support, or your peers may have empathy for your situation, but do not expect them to risk their liberty, livelihood and pensions for your abuse of powers. At the drop of a hat all cops will turn on a bad apple and they will stand in court and give evidence against you. I am not so naïve to think that there is not some corruption of this type out there, but from my experience this is usually found at an organisational level in the corridors of power where they are trying to protect the reputation of the force, there is no place for it on the streets.

Spare a thought for your supervisors, they have a hard juggling act to perform between managing staff welfare, managing work that needs to be completed and managing upwards and outwards to senior managers and the public. I have often seen supervisors turned on by members of their team because they have had to 'manage' the team member in a robust way, basically they have received a bollocking for not doing their job or for behaving in a manner that is not appropriate. Now this is why managers should not get too cosy and friendly with their teams, they need to keep a professional distance and be able to evidence their decision making and justify their behaviours. Once a supervisor steps into the realms of 'managing' a member of staff they enter a world of risk. Some officers do not have the resilience or character to accept that they were wrong and accept their bollocking, these are usually the 'Shift Hero' or 'sick, lame and lazy' types. What they will start to do is build a protective empire around them of people who they can manipulate in an effort to undermine the supervisor, they will try and evidence incidents in the past when the supervisor has done or said something inappropriate, they will also engineer situations to gather further evidence of this and undermine the supervisor at every opportunity. This behaviour to me just exposes the petty and childish nature of some people, if you ever have a true grievance don't drag the team into it, they may actually turn on you and support the supervisor for one thing, but it is also the incorrect and most destructive way to deal with your problems. Grow some resilience and have a one on one meeting with the supervisor, if you feel that you cannot do this then speak with another Sergeant or your Inspector, they will walk you through the situation and they will discuss what your options are in regard to starting the correct grievance procedure or acceptance that you were at fault. Supervisors are not usually stupid people and you will not be their first problem child, if they have challenged you about a performance issue they will have evidenced it in writing and linked a development plan to it. They have been forced into being formal about challenging staff because historically they have been unsupported by the organisation against staff that are being bitter and malicious, so, if you receive a quick bollocking for something or just get given a job you don't want to do, suck it up, buy the cakes for the team as a penance and move on, life is too short and the job is hard enough as it is without inside fighting or plotting.

Career Development

Many officers spend their whole career as a Police Constable and they are happy to work and stay in the same location for the entirety of their career, and there's nothing wrong with that. It's not how I would have liked to have spent my career, but for some people they are happy and content and they have no career aspirations of promotion or specialisation.

The Police service is a great place for variety, you can be a uniformed response officer one day, and then the next you can become an undercover operative who is infiltrating criminal networks. So, if you want to work towards promotion or a specialized role you need to start by putting a plan in place, you cannot become a career butterfly who jumps from interest to interest in various different roles. Some new joiners have their heads in the clouds and want to be a Superintendent with a gun, they watch TV shows like Line Of Duty and believe that you can get promoted really quick and still do all the sexy stuff like firearms, investigations and car chases. This is not the real world of career development in the Police. Here are a few tips on how to make the best of your career opportunities.

- Learn to be a productive and capable Police Officer, this sounds obvious I am sure, but you need to learn the basics of the job before you can fully understand any other role in the Police, this is why in the UK all student officers must complete 2 years probation before they are signed off as a competent Police Officer.
- Try before you buy, don't rush in to a role just because you thought you thought it looked exciting or sexy on TV. Ask for an attachment to the department, it may be that it doesn't live up to your expectations. Try attachments to other departments, this will help with networking and it will give

you a better understanding of what the other departments around you are doing. It will also validate why you do certain things or fill in certain risk assessment forms when you are out on response.

- If it is promotion you are after I suggest that you get as much experience in various departments beyond response. It is very sad to see people finish their two years probation and become an acting Sergeant straight away, they lack credibility and they lack sufficient knowledge of the organisation to become a competent supervisor. They also restrict their own career options too, imagine your career as a large triangle, the long base of the triangle being your experience and the sides as your rank. If you have a small amount of experience your base will be small and this restricts the size of your triangle, however, with a large base of experience your triangle is huge and you can put all that experience into different career pathways as you move through the rank structure. For example, PC Smith finishes their probation, gets promoted to Sergeant. A couple years later they decide that they want a Detective Sergeants job in child abuse, they do not have the sufficient experience, nor are they even qualified as a detective. So the now Sergeant Smith decides they will now become an Inspector, they struggle through the process as they are a one dimensional cop who has only ever worked in one area and only in a frontline uniformed role, let's be generous and say they pass. Inspector Smith has seen an advert to work within Operations as the Inspector for Firearms and the dog section, they apply for the job but yet again they have no relevant experience beyond that in their size restricted career triangle.

I know that is an extreme example and some people do get through and they can build their triangle, but this is not the norm and it is usually only restricted to those on accelerated promotion schemes, the rest of us have to battle our way through and take every opportunity we can. A career in the Police is a long one, enjoy it, don't feel like you have to chase the stripes and the pips, there are so many roles you can try for a few years then move to another role to gain more experience in another field. The unhappiest I ever was in the job was when I was trying to get promoted to the rank of Inspector, the constant back biting from other contenders, the pressure of gathering sufficient evidence to prove yourself, the rejection when you see people less able than yourself getting promoted for no other reason than they interview well or have connections in high places. I just hated it and I soon found my natural place as a Detective Sergeant, had I continued to try and be promoted I would have spent many years being stressed and unhappy at the person I was becoming.

You will change with promotion, you have to, you are moving into a leadership position. This means that you have to lead by example and you have to make decisions that can affect the careers of those around you. Some people will be unhappy at this change, they will want you to still be their mate and give them an easy time or some favouritism. Most people move stations when they are promoted to prevent the problems that come with familiarity. You may find that you were not ready for that promotion just yet, I have known acting Sergeants to hand back in their stripes as they couldn't do the job, they hated delegating tasks to people who they thought were their friends and getting grief for it, they lacked the experience to make sound decisions, they hated dealing with their teams welfare issues and the main one was that they missed being a cop, they didn't join to wipe cops noses and shuffle paperwork in the office, they joined to be a cop and lock up the bad guys. There is nothing wrong with handing the stripes back, it's not a failure, you were either not ready or not the correct person for that role, you must grasp it as an opportunity to get back to doing what you love or trying out your plan B in a specialised department.

- So, you want to be a detective? To do this you will have to most definitely have to get the first point squared away first, if you are not capable of being a good frontline cop then you will struggle as a detective.

  First thing to do is get yourself an attachment to an investigative team, it doesn't have to be the CID or a sexy Crime Squad, a lot of experience can be gleaned from a simple prisoner handling unit, these are the officers who deal with everything that is left in the cells in the morning with no one to take ownership of them. This job gives a lot of variety to your portfolio of experience, you will deal with anything from shop lifters all the way through to serious violent assaults. You will experience, interviewing, file preparation, liaise with solicitors of both the defence and prosecution and you will, learn how to quickly take an investigation to a positive outcome or quick closure if it's going nowhere. Prisoner handling teams are often bought in to bolster the strength of murder investigations too when they need extra resources.

As a detective you will have to pass the National Investigator Examination, this is a test that is as hard if not harder than the Sergeants exam and you will need to complete a portfolio of experience too, you will not receive any extra pay for this and you will still be a Police Constable, they will just call you Detective Constable, so no pay rise, no rank rise, but you will get status as a detective and exposure to better quality jobs, you won't be on crime scene guards, hospital bed watches and you won't be involved in as much public order type policing either.

Being a detective is not all about sharp suits and big cases, usually it involves long shifts, lots of paperwork and you are expected to investigate the most horrific incidents of violence and sexual abuse that many people do not know even exists on our streets. There is no one to hand the work over to either, a response officer can attend a job, arrest a suspect, do their statement and then walk away once its handed over. As a detective you do not have this luxury, you own it and you keep it until an outcome is decided.

- Take ownership of your career, no one else cares about your development, they may pretend they do but they don't, they care about their own. If someone's helping you to progress ask yourself why, are they genuinely helping you, or are they using you, they may actually be helping themselves by promoting someone from a diverse background and using it as evidence to get themselves promoted. If this does happen to you just make sure you get what you want out of the deal and accept it for what it is.
- Use the system to your advantage, being a good cop is not the only thing that will get you promoted or taken onto a specialised department. From the day you finish your time as a student officer ensure that you get your yearly performance reviews completed, evidence all the good stuff you have done and set out objectives for the year ahead. You can also evidence in these reviews your career aspirations and start a career pathway to where you want to be. In some quarters the performance review system has been called ineffective, I disagree, if nothing else it gives you an audit trail of your goals and achievements and it can be used to support you if you have a grievance with someone who won't let you progress in your career.

- Networking, you will need to get yourself known, if no one knows you then you have no chance of progression. You can do this by getting a name for yourself as a Thief Taker or a good cop, but you still need more than that, you can join associations or sports teams if you like, or become an expert in a certain field. but you need to become part of the fabric of the organisation. You can be a good cop, but being a good cop who represents the force at a national event looks better, it shows you care about your work and have bought in to the organisation.

Good Luck

Thank you for taking the time to read this guide, I could have written hundreds of chapters on multiple subjects, but then the guide becomes a boring and repetitive novel. I hope that this publication has entertained and informed you and I hope that you can take away from it some advice that has been given with good intent. It is exactly that, advice, if you don't want to take it that's fine, I am sure that you will soon navigate your way through your career either way. Some of you may have read this and have now decided that joining the Police is not for you, well that is a positive out take too. There are far too many people who have joined the Police to find out that it was not what they expected or that they didn't have the required resilience for the violence and long arduous hours that you are expected to work, if I have saved you that pain, you are welcome.

All that leaves me to say is good luck and I wish you all the best in your chosen pathway.

Other titles by the Author

'Hard Stop'

'A life of violence, crime & deception'

Available in all good book shops and on Amazon in hard copy, eBook and audible.

Contact the author

jackdawepublishing@gmail.com

Printed in Great Britain
by Amazon